I0831513

INDENTATION AND OTHER STORIES

ELMER HOLMES BOBST AWARD FOR EMERGING WRITERS

Established in 1983, the Elmer Holmes Bobst Awards in Arts and Letters are presented each year to individuals who have brought true distinction to the American literary scene. Recipients of the Awards include writers as varied as Toni Morrison, John Updike, Russell Baker, Flora Lewis, Edward Albee, Arthur Miller, and James Merrill. The Awards have now been expanded to include a category devoted to emerging writers of poetry and fiction, and in 1990 the jurors, E. L. Doctorow, Denis Donoghue, Galway Kinnell, and Richard Sennett, selected the first two winners in this category, Bruce Murphy, for his collection of poetry *Sing, Sing, Sing* and Joe Schall, for his *Indentation and Other Stories*. These two works are both published by New York University Press.

INDENTATION
AND
OTHER STORIES

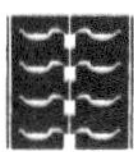

JOE SCHALL

NEW YORK UNIVERSITY PRESS
NEW YORK AND LONDON

Manufactured in the United States of America

Library of Congress Cataloging-in-Publication Data

Schall, Joe, 1959-
Indentation and other stories / Joe Schall.
p. cm.
ISBN 0-8147-7917-4 ISBN 0-8147-7918-2 (pbk.)
I. Title.
PS3569.C4732715 1990
813'.54-dc20 90-47338
CIP

New York University Press books are printed on acid-free paper, and their binding materials are chosen for strength and durability.

For Rob Funk

CONTENTS

INDENTATION AND OTHER STORIES

INDENTATION

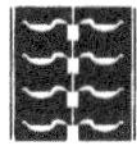

Donald David Sandborn read that twelve million Americans feared him so completely that they never came to visit. So he decided to beautify his apartment to attract tourists, to show the world he was a regular guy. Impression trays, he knew, should be the basic décor. Since everyone had a mouth, he reasoned, everyone would respond to impression trays with open grins. He had been taught that you had to appeal to all five of the senses if you hoped to create something aesthetic and alive. If handled properly, impression trays simultaneously activated all five of the senses, and they were set in a perpetual smile.

First, Dr. Sandborn bought forty-six sheets of four-by-eight pegboard at Claster's and ninety-seven packs of curtain hooks at K-Mart. He secured the sheets of pegboard to the walls in his apartment with six-penny nails. Then he gathered up his collection of impression trays, both disposable and nondisposable, and hung them from the curtain hooks in the pegboard. He arranged the attractive Temrex Rite Bite trays and Caulk Rim-Lock non-perforated water-cooled trays on the bathroom walls, because he knew that discriminating tourists judged the quality of a home by its bathroom. Naturally he hung the standard Super-Dent impression trays with retention rims in the living room, because they were the most pleasing to look at while you sat leisurely on the couch. He realized, though, that tourists were just as likely to be sitting while in the bathroom, so he had an aesthetic decision to make. Finally, he decided on the entire sani-tray assortment of Getz plastic disposables and the newest line of D-P Traten perforated plastic trays, and arranged them strategically across from the toilet at eye level, since they were both pleasing to the eye and had a more sanitary look than aluminum. From varying lengths of unwaxed floss, he tied a seemingly random assortment of F.G.P., Lactona, and Crown and Bridge trays, and attached these to hooks screwed into the ceiling tiles. They served as wind chimes when he opened all the windows or turned on all the fans. He realized that few of his tourists would be into impression trays on such an esoteric level as he, but he aspired to educate them gradually in a sublime manner.

Nine years earlier, Dr. Riddle had taught Sandborn not to take impressions lightly.

"Look at this, Sandborn," Dr. Riddle said, throwing down the May issue of *JADA* at his feet. The journal was open to a two-page ad: "Good Impressions: Making Them and Taking Them."

"This," said Dr. Riddle, "is your future battle. Taking and making good impressions. Come." Sandborn followed Dr. Riddle into his office and Dr. Riddle instructed him to sit back in the Belmont chair with the double-padded headrest.

"Open your mouth and pull your upper lip away from your teeth," Dr. Riddle ordered.

Dr. Riddle opened a jar of Jeltrate, scooped some powder into a wooden bowl, measured and mixed in 1/4 cup of boiling water, spooned the solution into a Baker's Edge-Lok impression tray, and jammed the tray into Sandborn's mouth, pushing up hard with his palm.

"Ehhsts stooo haoott," Sandborn said.

"Don't squirm, just watch," Dr. Riddle said, handing him a mirror.

Sandborn held the mirror in his right hand and kept the impression tray in place with his left hand. The mirror fogged up from the mist coming out of his mouth.

"What's wrong, Sandborn?" Dr. Riddle asked.

"Ah cunhh seah woth happena tumme, Dokka Real," he said.

"Then close your eyes and picture it. It's beautiful. You are taking your own impression. For the first time in your life you are taking charge of your own mouth. No instruments needed but your own two hands. No one else's fingers probing your privacy, no plastic gloves, no uv lights, no cotton swabs, no salivation, just your own, pure, steaming impression being taken by you."

"Wehn cun aha shhtop?" Sandborn asked.

"Look Sandborn," Dr. Riddle said, shoving another mirror in front of him. "This is your future. This is the staple of dentistry."

In the mirror, Sandborn's gums bled so badly that he could not see his impression.

"Now, let's do your lowers," Dr. Riddle said, reaching into Sandborn's mouth.

Knowing that mouth mirrors were a dentist's most basic visual aid, Dr. Sandborn reasoned that he could teach his future tourists to enjoy the sight of mouth mirrors if they got used to seeing them in a homey environment. So he purchased two gross of Autoclavable Reusable Glass Mouth Mirrors with rhodium coated lenses, removed the fiberglass handles with a soldering iron, then cemented the tiny, round reflectors in rows over all the former mirrors in his apartment. The bedroom mirror, shaped like an upside down scallop shell, was tricky, but he conquered the shape by cementing a small arc of mouth mirrors to the top of the shell and underlining it with ever-widening cemented smiles. Now, he thought excitedly, when any tourist looked into the new bedroom mirror, he would see a jagged replica of his own smiling face, and, stepping closer, would watch his face break into dozens of separate faces. Then, pressing his temple and cheekbone against the glass if he wished, he could inspect the image of his own reflection in his eyeball. This way, any tourist looking into Dr. Sandborn's mirrors secured instant friends. After just one tour, mouth mirrors would become funhouse mirrors.

He thought of everything. He went beyond the normal tour guide's duties. For instance, he placed a can of Dee Fog Spray on the bathroom and kitchen sinks, in case any tourists showered, shaved, or did the dishes. He supplied empty Starlite and Shofu boxes in the bathroom and bedroom so tourists could deposit their cosmetics, keys, and change in case of an overnight stay. He filled water bottles with Sparkl solution and lined them up on the kitchen counter next to a small cardboard sign: "If you want to have a water battle with another tourist, use Sparkl! It's safer and more hygienic than water, and it won't wrinkle your clothes." He scattered unmailed letters and Christmas cards addressed to patients on the coffee table, covering them with dentistry stamps, including the famous one depicting Henri Moissan and the two recent sets issued by Kuwait. And finally, for the *coup de maître*, he casually left *Atlas of the Mouth* opened to the pages on "Growth and Calcification Patterns of Enamel and Dentin," and propped the open book up in front of the television screen.

Seven years earlier, Sandborn had sat comfortably in Dr. Riddle's office chair.

"Listen to me, Sandbo. In one year you will be practicing. In one year I will have to call you doctor."

"Yes," Sandborn said.

"So you think you know it all? Now you've heard all about fissured tongues and subligual carbuncles so you think you're a hot property, right?"

"So they tell me."

"Who wrote *The Talking Tooth*?"

Sandborn continued to push the memory buttons on Dr. Riddle's chair, enjoying the soft, humming whir whenever the chair moved.

"*The Talking Tooth*. Who wrote it?"

"We didn't study that."

"And I'll tell you why you didn't study it. Because it's about pain. The real thing. Pain. You don't want to know about pain. Only money. I'll tell you who wrote it: Dr. Jim Cranshaw."

"*The* Jim Cranshaw?"

"His first book; a novel. The only real book he ever wrote. Before he sold out and started that chain of roto-dentists in shopping malls. I got a flyer last week about his latest scheme. Founding the first Amway for dentists. Every dentist is a shareholder. Dentists peddling products to other dentists for Christ's sake. An oral sensation. Word of mouth. DentAm. AmDent. DentAmerica."

"Sounds like a good idea," Sandborn said.

"Exactly. You think it's a good idea because you still don't understand what it's all about. Listen to this passage from *The Talking Tooth.* It's written from the perspective of a mandibular lateral incisor:

> "The lesion began as a small blister, but soon fine white lacy lines were radiating from the margin. They closed around me like a pillow and whispered promises into the night. Vainly I believed them, ignoring the violaceous papules that subtly crept over my body. I slept most of the day and drank most of the night. Finally I realized what was really happening to me. I screamed to have my entire area indurated.
>
> "Induration!" I screamed. "Induration or death!"

"That's easy," said Sandborn. "Wickham's disease. The lacy lines will soon be—"

"I'm not asking for a prognosis, Sandhead! I'm talking about the real thing! The lacy lines will be your patient's fingers wanting to close around your throat every time you go into a mouth! The screams you'll hear at night! The pain you'll never hear about! Don't you realize what I'm telling you, boy?"

"No," Sandborn said.

To appeal to the auditory sense, Dr. Sandborn provided a subtle alternative to elevator music—tapes that would be played suggestively in the background during the tour. He recorded some of the more popular TV shows with his VCR on the chance that the actors might make dental references, then rerecorded selected bits from the VCR tape onto a cassette tape, then remixed live from the cassette tape onto another cassette tape, dubbing in his own comments when appropriate, with a low-speed intraflex lux drill running serenely in the background. He began the tape with Fascinating Facts They Don't Tell You on TV. For instance, when Bill Cosby said "There's something berry crazy in the jello freezer," the commercial failed to acknowledge that Cosby was sitting comfortably in a dentist's chair at the time. Dr. Sandborn acknowledged it. When Johnny Carson ridiculed Dr. Mendelsohn's letter asking for kinder treatment of the dental profession, NBC failed to admit that Johnny's second wife divorced him because he ground his teeth at night—the real reason, Dr. Sandborn knew, why Johnny never told any bruxism jokes. Dr. Sandborn admitted it. Alex P. Keaton's comment that he preferred an evening of mime to an evening of dentistry posed problems until Dr. Sandborn simply switched the words "mime" and "dentistry." Surprisingly, some comments needed no editing, such as those by the dentist on M*A*S*H, who once avoided the latrine for eighteen hours straight and refused to kiss a nurse because of the germs. Of course, Dr. Sandborn excluded some material, such as Dick York's son boring a butterknife through a piece of toast to mimic a dentist's drill, and Dick getting his root canal atop a merry-go-round horse instead of in a proper dentist's chair, with the heavily moustached dentist wearing an absurd purple cape and dressed like David Copperfield. Some tourists, Dr. Sandborn knew, would misinterpret such information if it were included, and his tape would become counterproductive.

For the more hip kids and teenagers, he used Thomas McGuire's book, *The Tooth Trip*, reading aloud into a microphone from select sections of the book such as "A Day in the Life of a Germ," "The Bad Acid Trip," "Stimudents," "Your First Encounter with Chief White Coat," "Cavitron," and "How To Tell When You Have One." And, for the particularly squeamish, Dr. Sandborn read from Stolzenberg's *Psychosomatics and Suggestion Therapy in Dentistry*, with a Red Wing lathe running in the background to subliminally ease any tourist's lathe-anxiety.

"Did you ever realize," he read aloud, "that it takes more muscular effort to produce a frown than it does to produce a smile? The recent war produced many examples of physical disabilities which, basically, were nothing more than the physical expression of the mental fear of being exposed to danger in the armed services. In psychological terms, the suspicion attaches to every dentist, as it does to every surgeon, masseur, policeman, animal trainer, hangman, etc., that he *likes* his work. The public expects them to hate their work and engage in it with repugnance, or else be tarred with the brush of cruelty and sadism. So smile, it really makes a difference!"

Dr. Sandborn listened to the tapes over and over until they became white noise.

Five years earlier, Sandborn had sat in Dr. Riddle's dining room, eating the largest meal he had had in years.

"Taste this Sandy," Dr. Riddle said, shoving a forkful of bouillabaisse in front of Sandborn's mouth.

The bouillabaisse tasted like white rice with margarine. In fact, everything tasted like white rice with margarine, but there was no white rice with margarine on the table.

"Please dear, Mr. Sandborn looks full enough already," Mrs. Riddle said.

"So you think he's fat, do you?" Dr. Riddle said, poking towards Sandborn's belly. "The wife here thinks you're too fat."

"Thanks, I really am full," Sandborn said.

"You could stand to lose a few pounds," Mrs. Riddle said.

"Now let's treat our guest with some respect, dear. Tomorrow this boy graduates and goes into private practice with me."

"Oh yes," said Mrs. Riddle, "the great dental profession. Have you told him yet that you're manning a sinking ship? About the bile taste of bad breath? How you're going to create him in your own image?"

"Just the ticket Sandy, you and I opening our own office. Like a father and son."

"Do you know," Mrs. Riddle said to Sandborn, "why we don't have any children?"

"Did you know, Sandy, that Mrs. Riddle made this entire meal in the microwave?"

"That's very impressive," said Sandborn.

"That's why it all tastes like white rice with margarine," Dr. Riddle said.

Mrs. Riddle picked up her soup spoon.

"She's a microwave queen," Dr. Riddle said.

Mrs. Riddle scooped her soup spoon into a casserole dish and aimed carefully for her husband's mouth.

"Have some asparagus puff pie," she said gaily, sending it across the table and onto his forehead.

"Maybe I'd better be going," Sandborn said.

"Oh please do stay," Mrs. Riddle said. "For after dinner treats we have pumpkin bars and asparanuts."

Dr. Riddle pushed his chair back, squatted down, and lifted his end of the table, trying to slide the entire meal onto his wife's lap.

In the dining room of his apartment, Dr. Sandborn worked for thirty-seven evenings in a row, making informal placemats for the dining room table that the tourists could enjoy with him while they ate lunch. He laminated them himself. His plan was to serve the tourists in shifts of four to preserve that family feel without crowding anyone at the table. First, he reproduced a pencil sketch of Rembrandt's *The Charlatan,* depicting a market busker in sweeping criss-crossed and curved lines holding up a crude medicine with which to ease toothaches. This placemat was reserved, of course, for the artsy tourist. On top of it, the tourist might enjoy some cascadilla soup and perhaps some alsatian cheese salad, served with a tofu and soy sauce side plate.

The second placemat catered to the superstitious and neurotic tourist. It was a pen and ink drawing of Goya's *Hunting for Teeth,* with a woman standing on tiptoe averting her face and holding a scarf over it while removing the teeth from a man who had recently been hanged. Some women, Dr. Sandborn knew, still retained equally ridiculous superstitions about how to relieve their own toothache pain. One patient had told him that her mother used to make her eat a banana whenever she had a toothache. Invariably the girl would eat the banana and lose a tooth in the process. Any female tourist who might have had similar painful childhood experiences could sit at the Goya placemat and concentrate on the superstitious look on the woman's face, while sipping a hot soup completely unlike a banana, such as spicy tomato or mushroom bisque or even Brazilian black bean, if Dr. Sandborn had time to prepare it.

However, to show he was giving the ladies a fair shake, and in anticipation of the inevitable feminist tourist, he made a water color of Daumier's *She Stands Her Ground* for the third placemat, boasting a burly female dentist with her entire hand hidden in a patient's mouth, five overly sized molars and a tooth-key at her feet. He added just a touch of ruffle to the woman's dress at the shoulders, elbows, wrists, and waist to suggest a softer look than Daumier had. For the feminist tourist, Dr. Sandborn would prepare a regular ground beef hamburger on a plain Sunbeam roll with some ketchup, prudently holding the mayonaise, mustard, onions, pickles, relish, lettuce, tomato, cheese, and salt.

And, for the fourth placemat, geared to the particularly witty and analytical tourist, he pastelled a copy of the controversial 1956 painting by Solot, *The Revolt of the Molars,* using additive colors for the two adult forceps and subtractive colors for the two baby forceps. The forcep family huddled together on their handles behind the wall, terrified of being caught up in the bloody revolt outside, where a mob of molars hoisted some of the forceps' nuclear family members up onto the gallows, the molars dancing mirthfully. An intelligent eater, Dr. Sandborn knew, would recognize the placemat's symbolic representations of the crucial odontology issue: radical (tooth extraction) versus conservative (root canal). This placemat would be particularly relevant when serving bologna and cheese sandwiches.

He thought of everything. He decided against reproducing Elgström's 1945 water color, *The Widov,* depicting an old lady sitting in an office armchair and grinning reminiscently at her dead husband's false teeth smiling up at her from her hand. He even denied himself the urge to reproduce Pieter Breughel's 1556 *Christ Casting Out the Money-Changers,* completely resisting the temptation to circle the often-ignored dentist on Jesus's right with red crayon. The religious implications, he thought, would be too controversial. Also, he kept Paul Bunyans, sweet and sour pork, chili, sauerkraut, and pigs in a blanket strictly off the menu, because he knew what they would do to his tourist's breath.

Three years earlier, the two doctors had worked side by side in the same office.

"Smell this, partner," Dr. Riddle said, sneaking up behind Dr. Sandborn and covering his chin with a nitrous mask.

"Not me, your patient," Dr. Sandborn said, trying to stay calm and guiding Dr. Riddle's wrist to his patient's face.

"I'd rather be having a baby than a root canal," Dr. Riddle's patient said.

"Well here, Gladys, let me just adjust this chair a little," Dr. Riddle said.

Gladys laughed and breathed calmly with the mask over her nose.

Dr. Sandborn returned to the mouth of his own patient, twiddling his instruments like chopsticks, trying to scrape some plaque off a molar without frowning. The patient's breath smelled like yellow ammonia. Dr. Sandborn knew that was impossible. He knew because he had once answered a test question incorrectly: Antibacterial substances secreted in saliva include:

(a) lysozyme
(b) immunoglobulins
(c) peroxidase
(d) ammonia
(e) all of the above

He did detect, however, a hint of a yeasty smell, and he knew that was possible. All mouths, when opened, excreted a certain amount of yeast, merocrine, and something that smelled like vodka. The patient swallowed suddenly and Dr.

Sandborn caught a whiff of sour orange juice as the patient exhaled.

"Do you use mouthwash regularly?" Dr. Sandborn asked.

"No," the patient said.

"How long since you've had your teeth cleaned?" Dr. Sandborn asked.

"About five years," the patient said.

"No wonder you had curly little hairs stuck in there!" Dr. Riddle yelled from across the room.

Gladys laughed.

"This gas is great," she said. "I'm on a cloud. Floating down the highway with Frank Sinatra. He's singing 'Ring-A-Ding-Ding.' On a cloud."

"What flavor is it?" Dr. Riddle asked.

"Vanilla, silly, all clouds are vanilla."

"All good clouds are vanilla," he corrected her.

Dr. Sandborn tapped his own patient on the shoulder.

"Your mouth will taste funny for a while after this," he said, "but start using Listermint twice a day and the smell will go away."

"Okay," said the patient.

"Now," said Gladys, "the cloud is angel hair. Like at Christmas. And I'm taking a nap and eating an orange."

"What does it smell like?" Dr. Riddle asked.

"A lemon," she said, delighted. "The orange smells like a lemon!"

Dr. Sandborn had always been bothered by the stench of chicken or fish most people left lingering in their kitchens. He offered his tourists several instructive alternatives. Most dentists typically asked their patients to tap on articulating paper with their teeth, causing a foul odor of something which reminded Dr. Sandborn of camphor granules. He knew that if he asked his tourists to tap on articulating paper with their teeth at any point during the tour, most would leave. Instead, he placed an ashtub full of water between the stove and refrigerator, with strips of articulating paper floating freely on the surface and emitting a pretty blue bouquet. If a tourist ventured into the bathroom closet, he would find a special olfactory delight—a Baldor lathe running perpetually, with a generous mound of Fasteeth heaped into the aluminum splash and dust pan. He equipped the lathe with a number 9 acrylic bur and a peach stone for a more complete Fasteeth circulation than most tours would offer. After a few hours of the lathe running continuously, all the clothes in the closet were saturated with that unique polish and grind aroma.

In the bathroom Dr. Sandborn took special care, since he knew it was the most common room for household accidents. He placed a large plastic spray bottle of Campho-Phenique next to the band-aids and cotton balls and tongue depressors on the aluminum stand. Above the Campho-Phenique, he taped a sign: "Hey Kids! (and grownups too) This special solution smells remarkably like Chloraseptic, but do not spray it down the back of your throat or you will have to vomit and be rushed to the hospital. Do put it on cuts and bruises with cotton balls, then bring the dirty cotton balls to me. Enjoy the tour, Dr. Sandborn."

In the medicine cabinet, within handy reach of the sink, he planted a jar of orange sherbet-flavored Ultra-One for the kids, and unflavored Sensodyne toothpaste for the adults. On the bottle of Banicide on the bottom shelf, he wrote with a felt-tip: "For those who want to avoid spreading hepatitis, herpes, AIDS, and tuberculosis, gargle with this solution at least once every visit as soon as you enter the apartment."

In the living and dining areas, he perfumed the environment with open jars of Polyjel impression material and mint flavored Prophy Paste. Few dentists realized that Polyjel, once opened and aged for a few days, retained the scent of various fine cheeses, or that mint flavored Prophy Paste seemed much more spearmint than peppermint when one really concentrated on the fragrance.

Dr. Sandborn strolled around the apartment absorbing all the new smells, swinging his arms like a schoolgirl. Then he stopped, covered his eyes, nose, and mouth, and concentrated on breathing through his ears.

One year earlier, Dr. Sandborn begged Dr. Riddle to reconsider his decision.

"Touch my mind again," he pleaded. "Just hang around the office and do the books. I'll pay you."

"No Sandstorm," Dr. Riddle said quietly. "I've taught you all I can. If I retire now, the Mrs. and me can enjoy the money while we're still young enough."

"But you were right. I still don't understand pain. I don't know how to deal with it. My patients will stop coming if you don't stay."

Dr. Riddle touched his friend's shoulder. He spoke gently.

"There's something I've never told you. Remember the year I took the sabbatical? I was ready to crack up. I spent three months just pacing around in a church."

Dr. Riddle had paced the south aisle of the Wells Cathedral in Somerset every day, often with his eyes closed. When he thought that no one was around, he ran to the sculpture that he had read about with such fascination in the office. He reached up and stroked his fingertips over the capital of the stone column with his eyes shut, memorizing every feature. Years later, at night, he could conjure up the sculpture simply by closing his eyes: curved stone shoulders exploding out through torn concrete curls, framed by an elongated, linear face stretched taut and ragged at the left cheek by a finger, with a precise puncture in the open left eye where the pupil should have been.

"It looks like a gargoyle with a toothache," a woman had said from behind him, startling Dr. Riddle back to his senses.

"I bought a picture postcard of it for two pence at the front desk," she said, trying to put her hand into the sculpture's mouth.

Dr. Riddle had turned to her violently, thrust out his chin, and yanked the side of his mouth as close to his left ear as possible, closing his right eye viciously and flaring his nostrils like a dragon, looking, for an instant, exactly like the sculpture.

"How cute," the woman had said, snapping his picture. "My husband will love it."

According to the free tour brochure folded in Dr. Riddle's pocket, your pain would disappear if you touched Bishop William Bytton II's epitaph, engraved in the floor of the cathedral, and thought of the sculpture at the same time.

"So what happened?" Dr. Sandborn said excitedly. "Did it work?"

"I was arrested for sleeping on top of the epitaph," Dr. Riddle said. "Now goodbye."

"But I don't know how to act on my own."

"There's an old Chinese proverb," Dr. Riddle said. "If you want to be happy for an hour, take a nap."

Dr. Sandborn entered the empty spare bedroom of his apartment instinctively, without flicking on the light. This was the room in which his tourists were not allowed. In the middle of the dark floor, he practiced spinning around with his eyes closed without moving his feet, rolling his eyeshells within the perimeters of his head until they were soft as marbles. He clamped his teeth over his tongue so that he could cleanly taste the inside of a green inkpen. With a wallpaper paste brush and without moving his arms, he coated his body with red Eucerin and Neutrogena in the dark. Lacing his fingertips behind his head, he peeled on, one finger at a time, a pair of ambidextrous unisize disposable latex examination gloves, and decided he would never take them off. Then he lowered his body, from the neck down, onto a freshly ironed Kay-Pees professional dental beach towel, with medium-soft trubyte equalizing wax floating down from the ceiling and covering his body in layers of white licorice.

He exhaled silently and pictured his face in the dark. He had chosen his particular face because it had the perfect proportions according to the Greek criteria: five times the width of one eye and symmetrical features when one drew a line down the middle of the nose.

He prayed to Saint Apollonia in the dark, reading aloud from an overdue library book Dr. Riddle had loaned him:

Apollonia, Apollonia,
Holy Saint in Heaven
See my pain in yourself
Free me from evil pain
For my ache may torture me to death.

Apollonia is the patron saint of dentists. The Romans pulled all her teeth one at a time because she refused to renounce her faith. They broke her teeth with iron points, extracted the roots with tongs, and crushed her jawbone into chalk.

In the middle of the dark floor in the spare bedroom, Dr. Sandborn lay with a rag that had been soaked in chloroform draped around his face. He waited patiently for the tourists to arrive, breathing peacefully through his mouth.

THE PERILS OF ASTHMA

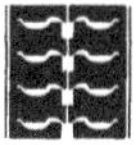

-1-
A Finch Named Goldy

Bub Lilly was certain of four things when he was twelve: he had acute asthma, he hovered between eighty-two and eighty-five pounds, he did not want to play the trumpet ever again, and he longed to own a Zebra finch and name it Goldy and let it fly free in his bedroom. Like cleats on a slow, spongy, indoor track, these certainties flopped around the perimeter of Bub's head, setting pace and direction for his life.

He spoke to his dad about it.

"Pop," he said, practicing the speech alone in his room. "I remember when I was eleven and you said a man should speak up when he's troubled or he would get crushed like a melon in his head for keeping it all inside or else it would all explode and that's what I'm doing and I'm telling you I will never never never ever play the trumpet again, and you will sell it for me and buy me a finch named Goldy and then we'll both be happy and men."

"Why would you name a finch Goldy?" his father would have said.

So Bub sat on his bed, his skinny butt crinkling the stiff green bedspread, and continued to heave with asthma, unsure about what to say to his father.

He sucked on his inhaler and decided not to tell him that he would never play the trumpet again yet.

Instead, the next day after band practice, Bub pretended that he threw his trumpet into the pond on the way home from school. Actually, he left it by the door in the band director's office—where the words "Mr. Gregory Bailey, Director," blared through the etched glass even at night when the school was quiet. Bub walked calmly to the edge of Garret's Pond, plucked the gleaming instrument from the plush mauve lining of his mind, thonked the mouthpiece into place, and sent the entire beast flickering and whooping through the sky with a sound like a mourning dove's retreat up, up, and out into the middle of the pond, where it hovered mystically on the water for a moment, then slurped down all at once, leaving behind only a black mysterious bubbling that made Bub grin knowingly.

While Bub stood looking at the pond, Mr. Bailey called Bub's mom and told her that her son was holding back the band.

"I'm afraid your son is holding back the band," he said. "And he left his trumpet in my office after practice."

"I'll talk to him," Mrs. Lilly said.

Mrs. Lilly yelled up the steps to her husband and told him that Mr. Bailey said Bub was holding back the band.

"I'll talk to him," Mr. Lilly said.

They all talked during dinner.

"More squash?" his mother offered, oozing it onto Bub's plate.

"Thanks," Bub said, "are there any more almonds?"

"Your father finished them all," she said, winking at her husband, signalling him to begin the conversation about Bub's holding back the band.

"I dropped my trumpet on the way home," Bub announced, suddenly sitting up straighter in his chair.

"When?" Mrs. Lilly said.

"After band practice. In Garret's Pond," Bub said.

"In Garret's Pond," Mr. Lilly repeated.

"In the pond," Bub said. "Definitely."

Mr. Lilly pensively crunched the fried almonds in his mouth.

"The case too?" Mrs. Lilly said, trying to hide a smile.

"No, not the case," Bub said, thinking fast. "Just the trumpet. And the mouthpiece. I left the case at school. In Mr. Bailey's office."

"Bub," his dad said, "Mr. Bailey says you're holding back the band—"

"Why did you leave the case at school?" Mrs. Lilly said.

"I forgot it," Bub said, looking down at his pasta. The white crescents were cold now and pocked with red pepper slices which Bub picked out and stuck in his pocket when his mom wasn't looking.

"I wanted to play it on the way home, so I forgot the case," Bub said, twiddling his fork nervously.

"Why are you holding back the band?" Mr. Lilly said.

"I don't know," Bub said, confused. "I don't know what it means. I wanted to play the trumpet on the way home, so I forgot the case, and I slipped and dropped it in Garret's Pond, and by now it's all rusted up I guess, and that's it."

Mr. Lilly noisily exhaled, sputtering his lips.

"Do you like being in the band, Bub?" his mother said.

"It's nice," Bub said, avoiding his father's eyes, "but the best part is the spit thing. I like to pull on the little plug and watch the spit run out. The more I play it the more spit there is. Sometimes I spit into the mouthpiece, hard on purpose, just so I can open it up and let the spit come out, but it doesn't work. I think the spit gets clogged up inside and comes out later when you don't expect it at all. It gets stuck in the coils or something."

"But do you like it?" his mother said.

Bub was quiet. He switched from his fork to his butterknife, feeling its weight in his hand. He felt suddenly bold, and wondered if it was a good time to mention the Zebra finch named Goldy.

"Playing the trumpet is good for your asthma," Mr. Lilly said flatly.

It was the old argument. Bub had a million retorts planned. It makes my head soft. It hurts my heart. It gives me diarrhea. Bullshit. Mr. Bailey is a queer. It's a waste of good brass. I feel more like a flute, Pop.

Bub gripped the butterknife tighter, blade-down, and looked over at his father's curved back. He could see the bulge of the spine through the crisp blue shirt. It would be so easy, he thought, to just go on over and poke him in the back with this knife and leave it sticking there while he falls flat on his face there in the plate. Then Bub imagined he would pick up the scattered almonds one at a time and stand there holding them happily between his teeth while his mother looked on, puzzled, asking him if he liked being in the band or not.

"I quit the band," he said, standing up.

"What? No," Mr. Lilly said.

"Tomorrow," Bub said.

"You're not," his father said.

"I'm quitting the band tomorrow and selling my trumpet for money," Bub said.

"Sit down, Bubba. You left the trumpet in Mr. Bailey's office. He called your mother after school."

"Tell him I quit," Bub said.

"No."

Bub shoved his chair behind him with the backs of his knees and walked away as slowly as he could stand it, waiting for the smack of his father's hand across the back of his neck. He climbed the stairs heavily, dragging one arm along the thick oak railing, his chest tightening with the first of the night's wheezes. Below him he could hear his mother, noisily clattering silverware as she cleared the table.

In his room the asthma hit harder. The wheezes came and went quickly now, getting ready to slow down and firmly settle like an engine in Bub's chest, chugging a steady, patterned lullaby that had periodically kept him awake at night since he was five. The lullaby was most pleasant when the engine ran slowly, so Bub relaxed his chest by turning out the light and standing a few inches from the wall, leaning his forehead against the poster his father had hung to inspire him when he was in the fourth grade. It was a reproduction of an aerial photograph of the 1980 Hilton Junior High School Marching Band, taken directly overhead from a helicopter which had been flown in special. Bub's father, a math teacher at Hilton Junior High, had helped Mr. Bailey design the formation. In the picture, Mr. Bailey sat comfortable and cross-legged in the exact center of the football field, flanked by tight, expanding circles of the ninety-seven band members sitting on the grass with elbows locked. They were all decked out in their new orange and mint green uniforms. For the coup de grace—

as Mr. Bailey told the photographer—the band members were surrounded by widening circles of supine musical instruments, organized by order of appearance in the Hilton alma mater, with the brass and woodwind bells all turned counterclockwise, and the bass drum at 12:00. The band members sat either back-to-back or foot-to-foot, all the smiles tilted up at the camera, the high fuzzy white hats forming jagged circles of their own, which layered down smaller and smaller to finally embrace Mr. Bailey's upturned face in expanding folds of cottony white love.

Bub didn't know that his father had helped to design the poster, but he still sensed that it had some odd historical power over him. When he slept, a car's headlights occasionally arced along his bedroom wall and the fuzzy white hats gave him two long secret winks.

In his room, Bub rocked familiarly from side-to-side on his forehead against the poster, faintly aware of some memory of dinner stuck in his throat, catching fragments of the conversation downstairs between wheezes.

His own mind. Lips. A little nervous. Practice, practice. Asthma too. Walks around puckering. The paper route. Quit the band. Acting up. His own head. I know.

They were talking about him, Bub knew. He could tell that he and his mother had won by the lowering volume of his father's voice. Soon all he heard was the slowing pull and release of the asthma engine in his chest. He reached a comfortable rhythm, getting to where he pretended there were tiny bunches of bubbles packed into the pasta crescents lying somewhere beneath his lungs. With each exhale he managed to release a few bubbles at a time, which rose up to scrape and tickle his throat, then escaped out onto the bed, where they popped and left small damp circles. Now he would be able to fall asleep if he propped himself up on an extra pillow. Now he could pull down the poster and lean his forehead against the blank, cream wall.

Tomorrow, he decided firmly, he would quit the band, take the trumpet to the pet store, leave it by the birdcages, and carry Goldy home in a tiny, fold-out, colored box.

-2-
No Sheetin Way

The next day was Saturday, so Bub couldn't quit the band, but his dad stood talking to him in the living room about it anyway. Bub knelt on the floor, folding the newspapers, while Mr. Lilly talked.

"Being in the band is your own business, I guess. Quit if you want, but let's just get one thing settled right now. If you want to quit the band you're on your own with it. I can't go to Mr. Bailey for you. He's a friend and a colleague. He'll be surprised, and I'll be the one who he stares at. You've got to do it and tie it all up yourself. Like a package."

He waited.

"Okay," said Bub.

"Now next week is the first football game. So do yourself and Mr. Bailey and the whole team a favor and quit on Monday morning first thing if you're going to do it. If you're going to go through with it that's the right way. Or else you should at least stick out the season. And don't expect me to quit for you. Like with the Boy Scouts. Not this time."

Bub had stopped folding his papers and was just staring at his father's mouth, sort of entranced by how the lips never quite seemed to close, yet moved around far too much on the face, always a few utterances ahead of themselves. He knew when his dad was about to end a speech because an odd sort of punctuation started creeping into his lips. A dash here. Two periods in a row there. Something similar to a sputter or a tentative throat-clearing or the beginning of a muffled cough. Any one of these was a sure trigger to Bub that his dad was through thinking up things to say for awhile.

"And Bubba," Mr. Lilly said, stepping back gently into the stairwell, "your Mom and I talked it over and if you still want to I hope you won't feel like I pressured you into going in in the first place. I know it's not like the army or something, where you have to join up. I think, that is I hope, I didn't really talk you into something. You didn't want to do it anyway, that's okay."

"Okay," said Bub.

"Now let's get those papers out," Mr. Lilly said, sort of mussing up Bub's hair in his mind.

Bub hiked the two *Hilton Times* paperbags over his shoulders, ran down the porch steps, and rode off on his bike, happy to be away from the house and outside the circumference of his father's voice. He turned down the alley in the middle of the block, thinking that there were probably only about ten paperboys in all of Hilton, and some of them were girls.

His paper route was the most unpredictable thing in his life. Every day he guessed the number of pages that he thought would be in the paper, and almost every day he was wrong. On the day before Thanksgiving of the previous year, the paper had been quadruple-thick because of the Christmas advertising, and Bub was off by fifty-six pages. He had to make two trips and his shoulders were sore for three days.

But there were victories as well. Using the thumbs-turn method, Bub could fold a paper in three seconds, with the empty white spaces between the columns matching up exactly to the folds. He could read the front page in under seven minutes, and usually found at least one typo with ease. With his friend Spotty's help, Bub could do his own half of the route in under thirty minutes.

He stopped his bike and waited in the alley behind Spotty's house.

"How many today, Booble?" said Spotty, skidding his back tire neatly up to within a few inches of Bub's. He rarely called Bub by his given name, but delighted in coming up with variations and testing out the reaction. "Booble" was a brand new one which Bub completely ignored because he had no idea what it might mean.

"Thirty-two," said Bub, lifting one of the bags over his head and handing it to Spotty.

"I knew it! Absolutely," said Spotty. "Every third Saturday."

"You didn't know it," Bub said quietly, uncertain.

Spotty's real name was Scotty, but he had nicknamed himself Spotty two years before because of his tendency to freckle, and the name had stuck. Even Mr. Bailey called him Spotty.

"So you're really quitting," Spotty said, incredulous, hoisting the bag over his own shoulder.

"Yup," Bub said. "First thing Monday."

"No way sheet," said Spotty. The printer's ink from the bag strap had smudged a neat curl across his pudgy chin, but Bub didn't tell him. "No sheetin way. Bailey Boy will have a turd. An outright turd. Right there in the bandroom."

"A turd and a half," Bub said, confident.

"No sheetin way."

"It's definite," Bub said. "I told my dad even."

"To hell you did. Two turds at least."

"Yup."

"You told your father, no freakin sheet? Mister Math. I'll bet he cussed you out."

"No way."

They straddled their bikes side by side in the alley, tips of the handlebars touching, looking like ludicrous fraternal flesh and metal twins with a bulging sac at opposite hips.

"I'll bet he railed your Buttinski. A wall shot. I can see it now."

"Nope. He told me it was a package for Bailey Boy. A favor. That the band isn't the army. My dad is weird."

"Your dad is *gay*," Spotty said. "No freakin way. You're definitely sheetin my ass. Spank my monkey. Spank it."

"You're a queer," Bub said.

Right away he knew he shouldn't have said it. Spotty was pretty fat, Bub knew. He was almost fourteen, outweighed Bub by over seventy pounds, and his bike reached two inches higher and was a BMX. It also cost fifty-two dollars more. Bub noted most of this, with far less precision, as Spotty tried to sort of jump off his bike and punch Bub in the chest all in one motion. He ended up kicking his own bike over onto Bub's, his foot caught under the pedal, and they all sprawled together into an unruly heap on the stones. The neatly folded papers formed a slowly growing island around them as the two boys squirmed together briefly, then Spotty tightened his hold around Bub's chest and someone's sissy bar. It was their fifth fight.

"Take it back Bubbowl."

"You're a freakin queer."

"Take it back Sally."

Bub weakly kicked his feet against Spotty's ankles a few times, then, in a sudden gasp, the engine in his chest churned and the asthma took over. Wheeze in. Wheeze out. Wheeze in. Out. Wheeze in was always first. Bub didn't know why.

"Lemme up. I got asthma."

By now Spotty was half sitting, half lying, on his own front tire and Bub's stomach. The rim of Bub's back wheel nearly bent from all the shuffling weight. A woman with two big bows of hair framing her head stood watching them from the mouth of the alley, a Chow Chow straining at the leash in her hand.

"Take it—" Spotty said, shifting his weight and nearly cracking two of Bub's spokes "—back."

"Okay. Okay," Bub wheezed. "King. You're the king. I was kiddin. Spot. You're. The main. Monster." Bub wheezed in hard and high-pitched so Spotty would hear it.

Spotty loosened his hold but made no move to get up. Their fights usually ended this way.

"Let me. Up. You're. Prince."

"Hold your breath."

Bub held his breath while Spotty floundered off him and picked up his bike. The woman with the two big bows walked on, losing interest, but the Chow Chow kept glancing back.

"Okay, let it out," Spotty said, starting to worry. "Careful."

Bub let out his breath, the center of his chest pinching coldly, and remained sitting on the frame of his bike, gradually slowing his breathing down.

"Where's your inhaler?"

"The freakin thing. Doesn't help."

"Is it better?" Spotty said, breathing heavily himself.

"I need to get. A little more. Rhythm," Bub said. "Like. A train. Just starting. To go. Like. In the movies. Listen. To the train. Go. That's just. How it is."

"What about when it speeds up?" Spotty said, getting interested.

"The train? Or me?"

"The train."

"Then," said Bub, "I can't hear it. Anymore."

"Oh," said Spotty, confused. He puzzled over Bub's answer a few seconds. "You're a freakin queer."

Bub continued to wheeze. He righted their bicycles and gathered the papers back into the bags while Spotty surveyed the damage.

"Two torn papers. One shirttail out. Your chain's off. Grease all over your pants."

"We'd better. Get going," Bub said.

"Hang on. I scratched your neck a little. A stone in my pocket. Three dimes on the ground. One penny. An asthma attack. And a partridge in a pair of trees."

Spotty grinned at Bub comfortably. He was his elder, his conquerer, his paper partner, his pal.

Silent, Bub slipped his chain back over the sprocket and wiped the grease from his fingers onto his paperbag, almost obliterating the "l" in "Hilton."

"You got an ink smear. On your chin," Bub said.

"Thanks," said Spotty, wetting his palm with his tongue and wiping it under his mouth.

"Hey, are we still Bubs?" Spotty asked, holding out his hand for Bub to slap.

"Still Bubs," Bub said, lifting his leg over his bike seat.

"Hey Spotty—" Bub said quietly, slapping the outstretched palm with a crack. "Go."

Bub pedalled off, hooting and kicking stones behind him, while Spotty struggled onto his own bike and sputtered. "Aw, no freakin freakin fair. Bubblebutt. Bowser. Sheet you. Pussy willow. Pussy."

Bub ground the words out with his straining legs as he sped towards his half of the route, while Spotty puffed his way along in the opposite direction, vaguely curious as to how the asthma had gone away so fast. Bub's half of the route had four big hills and Spotty's had only one, but Spotty had more traffic to dodge and there was a donut shop on Front Street. He usually got a chocolate eclair, and sometimes a Tahitian Treat. Bub made no stops, and usually finished passing first. The winner got to hard-knuckle the loser one time for each minute the loser was behind him. Sometimes Bub waited twenty-five minutes behind Spotty's house before he showed up. He would practice hard-knuckling on the leaves of a small Maple tree in Spotty's backyard.

As Spotty stood looking through the glass case, puzzling between Bavarian cream and white cream, Bub hummed his way down Pike Street, completely unaware of how numbers and words were continuing to form a higher, more meaningful heap in his life. His paper route and recent aspirations and asthma competed for his mental space: Corders. Kleins. Be a freakin rock star. Littles. What a stupid name. Klines. Wheeze in. On the porch over the rail into the freakin wall. Goldy. Definitely. Named Goldy. On Monday. Across the street. Wilsons. Phoney company. Over the stone hill. Bam. And bam. Knuckle the hell out of him. Four in a row. Sky hook. The freakin old bag in the ugly green house. Kimmels. Tuttles. Freakin mailbox. Goldy.

Forty minutes later, Bub got to give Spotty twelve hard-knuckles. The last one took a little bit of skin. Spotty shook the sting from his hand, excitedly telling Bub the news.

"I'm quittin too Bub. I'll quit with ya. Screw the flute. I don't give a flying frick about the flute. I'll tell Bailey Boy I got a disease."

"AIDS!" said Bub.

"Yeah, yeah, AIDS. That'll scare him off. He won't touch

me. He'll throw the flute in the freakin garbage. Freakin AIDS. He'll have a fricking frog. Outright."

"Wait, wait, wait. I got it," said Bub, holding up one finger profoundly. "Tell him he can blow the flute himself."

"Yeah, yeah! You're a genius, Boo-Boo. You can freakin blow it freakin yourself Bailey Boy. Freakin-A."

"You can Saran Wrap it for all I care," Bub said.

They chortled together for awhile, Bub theatrically falling off his bike with laughter, then they made more specific plans. Both boys agreed that they should quit separately on Monday so that Mr. Bailey couldn't try to talk them out of it. Somehow, they figured, he would be much more stunned by two separate quittings on the same day, and would probably be left in a comical state of speechlessness.

Swelling with dreams of band-freedom and a docile Mr. Bailey, Bub and Spotty split like two jets behind Spotty's house—not knowing that the real reason two such able pilots couldn't face quitting the band together was because each one would be waiting for the other to do the talking—not knowing that the real reason they wanted to quit was because of the odd quivering in their shoulders when the instruments got heavy, and the blank look that Mr. Bailey gave them as if they were large potatoes propped in their chairs, and the strange scariness alive within that wide stretch of noise when the whole bandroom tuned up all at once.

-3-
They're All Odd Numbers

Mrs. Lilly's first name was Lillian. She had no middle name. In the beginning, she had toyed seriously with the notion of refusing to marry John because of the last-name issue.

"If only it was the other way around or something," she had said quietly when she was twenty-three. "Lilly Lillian sounds better than Lillian Lilly at least. It's all backwards."

"So you go by Lill," John said, shrugging and twiddling one end of his moustache, an hourly habit in those days. "And nobody notices. Not backwards at all. Perfectly natural. Lill Lilly. Sounds very sure of itself. Confident. Like a President's wife."

He chuckled lazily and cuddled closer to her on the couch, but she wasn't quite convinced. Nothing was wrong with her own last name, she supposed out loud, and maybe it wouldn't be so strange if they both took on her name instead of his. It was 1969, she argued—people were *ready* for radical things to happen. But John pointed out again that her current last name—Smith—would end up being silly and embarrassing for them both, especially at the wedding.

"Ladies and gentlemen," John said, standing up in front of the couch and blessing the congregation in imitation of a priest, "it gives me great pleasure to present to you, for the first time in history, Mr. and Mrs. John Smith. Applause, applause."

Lillian didn't clap along, but managed a grin.

"Then," John said, "they'd give us enough bus fare to explore Virginia on our honeymoon. Someone would slip me a little pickax and a compass and a condom at the reception, and you'd turn into a fat old prairie-wife."

He guffawed, delighted with his articulate wit.

"What about a different last name?" Lillian suggested. "Like Esterhaus or Stockholm. Something foreign. What about our kids?"

Then John explained carefully, squaring his shoulders and using both hands to shape his point in the air, that his father was a Lilly, his mother was a Lilly, and so on, and he wasn't about to snub his parents or defect to another country or even *talk* about children just yet, and thus ended their first real tiff.

Two days later when they went to the courthouse to get the marriage license the last-name issue was all settled, and a smiling woman handed them their license and a congratulatory Newlywed Gift Pax—a drawstring plastic bag stuffed with one tube of Crest, a six-ounce bottle of Tide, some generic cologne, a sampler of Stayfree Minipads, two Tampax tampons, six caplets of Midol Maximum Strength, a packet of food and car coupons, and two Massengill disposable douches.

Lillian was responsible for taking care of the Gift Pax, as she was for ordering the flowers, choosing the wedding music, and filing for the name change. In a pensive mood a week before the wedding, she dumped the insides of the Gift Pax bag out onto her bed when her parents weren't home and arranged everything into categories. The contents of the largest pile, she realized, had been chosen for a woman, aimed at some mythic deirrigation that was to be a natural part of her life to come. The messages stamped on the items were unescapable—"Open This End" and "Do Not Flush" and "It's Easy"—the same cadences and commands she'd been marching to for ten years, since she'd first noticed her body emptying itself against her will, but now it was all somehow intimately connected with John. Tiptoeing barefoot like a naughty adolescent boy, she chose a tampon and one caplet of Midol from her pile, took them into the bathroom, and filled the sink with water. Dropped in the sink, the tampon burst out into a languid white butterfly-shrimp, while the Midol steamed up into mystic fragrant pebbles, eventually finding their way into the white fluff. This was what womanhood must be, she thought—floating around bloated with bits of debris clinging to you, until finally the weight made you sink. Or lying dormant, dissolving away into white space—silent while the world watched; suspicious that what really mattered was that a woman learn to properly stanch and flush her own blood, to embrace both the vitality and the ugliness of her flesh. Lillian paced around the upstairs rooms, swinging her arms—feeling herself a lonely teenage girl, emptied of all that was dreamy or glorious. She lingered in the bathroom and leaned her head against the cool window, breathing mouthwash mist onto the frosted glass. She thought about calling off the wedding, or asking John to somehow prove his love, or at least demanding that he learn to poke fun at his last name.

After she and John had been married for two years, Lillian developed a secret fondness for her new name, saying it aloud over and over with her hands sunk to the wrists in warm, sudsy dishwater, enjoying how the name jaunted and clicked between the teeth and the palate. She stared into the little lemony bubbles nestled into a teaspoon and delighted in watching her lips say the name upside down.

She got to the point where she could say the name, over and over, without noticeably moving her lips. For the first time, she wondered if she had the stuff to be a ventriloquist. She noticed that only the "Lill" part of the name required her to expel any air. When she was pregnant with Bub, something seemed cozy and instinctual and dogmatic about bobbing her head slightly as she repeated the name, and during her labor it all became her mantra, her cradle, her "Lillian Lilly Lillian Lilly Lillian" way of rocking herself through childbirth.

John greeted Bub's birth with far less certitude.

"Why doesn't he moan or something? He's too quiet," John said, scowling and nervous. He laid his son's four-hour-old little body in the crook of Lillian's arm and leaned over the hospital bed a bit nearer to her lips. The woman in the next bed coughed loudly.

"They said they're going to put him on a respirator," John whispered confidentially. "What's wrong with him?"

Lillian tilted her head on the pillow and looked at his face, gingerly stretching out her lips a bit as he kissed her. The moustache was gone now and had been replaced by several tiny pinches in the upper lip. John's one of those people, she thought, whose lips you just never really notice until the moustache is gone. The moustache had made him droopy-mouthed and serious, but its absence revealed new edges to his smile and a squirminess to his mouth that Lillian had never imagined. She learned how to grin as she kissed him.

"Piss," said the woman in the bed next to Lillian's, turning on her side to face the Lillys.

"Don't worry hon," Lillian said. "He's just delicate. Like a flower. Like a wet new flower. He'll be fine sweetie, he'll be fine."

"They said his lungs aren't big enough yet," John whispered. "He's breathing through his nose, I think. Listen."

"He's okay." Lillian stroked her husband's forearm. Bub had already spent fifteen minutes clutching her pinky finger in his fist, crying and squirming in healthy little jerks, and she knew he would be all right.

"*Pissss,*" the woman insisted, sitting up in her bed. "I stink like shitty, shitty, *pissss.*"

John looked over just as she struggled her hospital gown off her front, revealing coin-sized purple blotches dotting her sides, her skin folding downward in a pattern that suggested her body was dripping away into a slow, patient puddle.

"Get these damn things off me," she said, scratching up and down her sides, squinting directly at John. "Get them. Off."

John looked away and stared down at his own son, who was as buoyant and fat as a puppy.

Bub was on the respirator for two days, and they had to listen to his breathing carefully at home for about a week.

"I think he's groaning a little," John said anxiously, sitting on the couch at home, holding Bub against his shoulder to burp him. "I heard him gurgle, sort of, but it wasn't like a wet sound or anything, it's like he has a little pebble stuck in there. A couple of pebbles. It was a groan, sort of."

"He's fine," Lillian said, gazing at them both dreamily from across the room. This was her favorite part of motherhood—the watching. She had never seen John so childlike, so worrisome. If Bub sputtered a little of her breast milk out of his mouth, John wanted to call the ambulance. If Bub frowned hard John laid him on the carpet and stuck his ear to the small chest to make sure the heart was still beating. Inside Bub's chest, he could hear a perfect, pumping cadence, with just a touch of congestion rolling around once in a while—"It's like, like a tiny tumbleweed that blew off course," John told Lillian excitedly, "but it sounds healthy too, just blowing around happy there, warm and safe. A good sound. An ocean." Lillian had never known her husband to be quite so imaginative and childlike, and she loved to sit back and watch.

But sometimes his imagination failed him, and John felt at a complete loss with Bub.

"*You* burp him," he would finally tell his wife, carrying Bub by the armpits across the room. "You do it better."

"I *hear* him burp better than you do, that's all."

"What does it sounds like to you, anyway?"

"I do it like the dolphin," Lillian said, patting Bub's back. She had recently become vegetarian, and used animal metaphors generously. "I use my sonar to find the air bubble, and poke it right up out of him with my long nose."

Bub eeped out a burp in confirmation.

"That kid is turning you weird," John said, shaking his head and walking off.

Lillian had to admit it was true. Since she'd had Bub, she'd been getting weird. She had cravings now not for juices and popcorn and carob, but for words and facts and cleanliness. She'd spend hours at a time just on the letter "p"—musing over the definitions of words like "plaid" and "plutonium" and "pluvial"—fascinated that she and Bub were just along for the ride, while all the words were out there reverberating somewhere near the stratosphere whether anybody liked it or not. She told Bub about some of the words when they were alone the way some parents sing softly to their children long after they've fallen asleep.

Facts were no less fascinating for Lillian, but pure trivia was useless. Facts were those things which had historical significance but were usually misunderstood—like the fact that Henry the Eighth, infested not with a burning groin but with bleeding gums, had not really died of syphilis but of scurvy—probably as payment, Lillian thought, for hoarding mountains of meat—and the fact that the four gospels for the New Testament were selected by a timid monk with a facial tic in the south of France, and the fact that Isaac Newton really *did* get hit on the head with an apple, forcing the thing that fixed Lillian's feet to the earth to be set into motion. She sought a similar kind of motion through cleaning. She cleaned their apartment with ruthless abandon—adding or removing smells almost daily—resting Bub on her hip while she dumped something pine-scented into a bucket or sprinkled baking soda over the carpet. When the apartment was finally filled with enough of the cleaning smells, she would sit on the rocker with Bub and smell everything and not talk at all for awhile.

After twenty-three months of perusing, with Bub at her side, most of the weirdness she could find, Lillian agreed with John that it was time she did what she was trained for and she took a job teaching social studies at the Hilton Senior High School. Fridays in her classroom were devoted entirely to facts.

John's story was entirely different. Along with Bub's birth and Lillian's flair for weirdness came John's new-found imagination, usually spilling out of his lips in strange half-metaphors, sawed-off similes, and quasi-clichés. He couldn't quite squeeze his imagination shut; selectivity wasn't important as long as he had an audience, and his usual audience was either his eighth grade class of inattentive algebraists or a skinny, starchy-smelling Bub. If John thought of something to say he said it. And what he usually thought of were things tactile, wistful, and tawdry. Like a huge brown shopping bag with no writing on it. Like short lengths of rope knotted together into two legs of a monstrous nearly-equilateral triangle. Like spit on a skewer. Like the name "Bub," which John had chosen himself.

Such inspirations occurred suddenly to him and just as suddenly he gave them birth through speech, dropping them out on the ground where one of his students or Bub or any passerby could give them a quick once-over. But as Bub grew, John seemed to have less and less time to think of things to say, and before he knew it Bub was six years old, then seven, then almost eight and John hadn't told him even half of what he meant to yet.

He made up for some of the lost words while Bub was in the hospital recovering from his first bad asthma attack. He sat at the foot of his son's bed for hours, explaining to him that

Lillian was at a P.T.A. meeting and would be in to see him afterwards, and that he had bought Bub a trumpet for his eighth birthday, which he could learn to play the same way Ali boxed if he practiced hard enough, and that they were getting a specialist in to see him who knew every cough in the book; Bub half-listened and smiled and was glad to just lie down for a few days and not have to think about anything but the mysterious illness budding in his chest, which didn't hurt really as much as it reminded him that he was breathing all the time.

When the doctors agreed that Bub simply had plain old asthma, which had, in this case, combined with a virus to form a bad bronchial cold, Bub's doctor—Maynard Masters—had a private talk with Mrs. Lilly.

After five minutes of restraint, Doctor Masters finally got to the point.

"When you breastfed him, did you switch back and forth from the bottle to the breast at random, or were you careful to be consistent?"

Lillian thought about throwing out her arms and raising her whole chest at him defiantly, as if this would be evidence enough that her son had been properly nourished since birth and that Bub's asthma had evolved in his own chest, not hers. Instead she just shuffled around in her seat.

"He hardly touched the bottle until he was almost one-and-a-half," she said. "Until he started making sounds like words."

"Good."

"We're lactovegetarians," Lillian said, trying to sound superior. She wanted to show him up on at least one thing—this man whose name sounded like a half-hearted apology and who, since she'd sat down, had been twisting apart paperclips and dropping the segments in meaningless patterns on his desk. She was half expecting him to accuse her of weaning Bub on spinach and peanuts, or claim that her breast milk ran green, but the doctor just gave a quiet satisfied "Hummph."

"So he gets lots of milk and eggs," he said. "Cut back on them. They could be irritating his bronchial passages, and too much cow's milk could flare up some wheezier bronchitis and some recurrent otitis media later on."

"What else?" said Lillian, trying not to feel one-upped, and thinking of letting out a quiet "Hummph" herself.

"He should watch out for dust. Keep his room clean. Maybe get an air cleaner. Steer clear of pets. And we'll test him for allergies while he's here."

Lillian felt a little like Doctor Masters had just put in a bid on her house.

"And give him a hamburger once in awhile," the doctor said, standing up and sticking out his hand jovially. "There's nothing wrong with a little protein."

"Go to hell," Lillian said.

A few hours later, John and Lillian stood together next to Bub's hospital bed and explained that it was just asthma—nothing to worry about and easy to outgrow—and that Bub would be home soon and blowing on the trumpet for therapy and changing his diet some maybe. John held up a chart that he and Doctor Masters had drawn up together. The chart, he explained, told Bub how many anti-asthma pills to take once he got home.

PREDNISOLONE DOSAGE: 5 mg

DAY:	1	2	3	4	5
Morning	4	4	2	1	0
Afternoon	5	4	1	1	0
Evening	4	2	1	0	0

"So now," John explained to his son, "we have a plan. You just take these little pills like on the chart and you're all better. And we keep an eye on your chest. We're all set."

"You'll be fine," Lillian said, squeezing Bub's hand.

Bub stared at the chart for awhile.

"They're all odd numbers," he said.

"What?"

"When you add them up," he said, pointing to the piece of paper dangling in front of him from his father's hand, "they're all odd numbers."

"Across or up and down?" Lillian said.

"Across."

John quickly checked Bub's math and nodded his head. "Good boy."

"Now get some sleep, sweetie," Lillian said, kissing his forehead. His father squeezed Bub's hand and pulled down the chain above the bed, leaving only a flat layer of fluorescent light spilling in from the hallway and crossing Bub at the ankles.

"Good night," he said to their silhouettes.

Nobody moved for a moment.

"Mom," Bub whispered, "how many days till I'm eight?"

"Two."

"Will I be home then?"

"Yes. Promise."

"Know what?" Bub said. "I got asthma when I was five." He had been waiting all day to tell them. Now that this thing he'd been aware of for a long time had a name, he wanted to give all the parts of the asthma a name. The part that made a coiling sound in his sinuses needed a name. The part that turned things over in his lungs needed one too, probably the same one that would be given to the little hand that crawled around inside and tickled his throat. But the part that most needed a name was the one that enabled him to bring forth, almost any time he wanted, a tremendous raw bark from his chest, which he usually cupped in his hands or muffled in his pillow because he liked to feel how powerful it was.

"No Bubba," John said quietly. "You haven't had asthma before. Just a couple days ago."

"I was five," Bub insisted. "I had it. At least twice. And then again when I was seven. I still am seven. I didn't know what to do. I stayed in my room. But it was a long time ago. I just never told you." Bub was still whispering. He liked to whisper in the dark.

"It's okay. You're okay now," Lillian said.

"I didn't know what to do," Bub said, relieved to finally be telling them, "so I just sat down and waited, and I breathed and coughed, and finally my chest went to sleep. That's what happens. My chest goes to sleep."

Mrs. Lilly smiled in the dark, as if she and Bub were sharing an old secret. She thought maybe her son would be an artist.

"Get some rest," she said. "You're a good boy."

She and John walked out, and Bub lay thinking about how the asthma had made his chest go to sleep ever since he was five, and wondered what would happen if his stomach and his legs and even his feet went to sleep all at the same time.

The boy in the bed next to Bub's couldn't sleep.

"Hey kid?" the boy whispered. "Did your bowels move today?"

"What? When?"

"Your bowels. The nurse asked me if my bowels moved today. Did yours?"

Bub pictured tiers filled with black and swirled bowling balls, like the ones where his father bowled, suddenly tipping and emptying all the balls off onto the floor.

"I don't know," he said.

"Me neither. I said 'no way.' She said they're gonna haveta feed me jello. What does it mean?"

"I don't know," Bub whispered, the words sounding flat and small and permanent in the dark.

"I'm going home this weekend," the boy said.

"I'll be eight in two days," Bub said.

Bub turned on his stomach and eventually forgot about his chest and stomach and legs and feet going to sleep, and he stopped hearing the clacks of bowling balls against each other. Instead, something funny happened in his head. During the next few years, it would happen again and again during the oddly suspended moments just before sleep, but this was the very first time it happened. On the black and pink screen of his closed eyelids, Bub began to see things. He saw a tiny flat man in a hat who suddenly inflated and bulged big, then a rounded gray elephant which zipped down into a black dot, then dozens of undersized balloons that burst into silent startling circles. He sensed somehow that these things belonged to sleep, and that they belonged only to *his* sleep. Nothing else could have them. Nothing else could quite know the puzzling lilting going on in the dark spaces before him, and Bub would never try to tell anyone about it. It was his, and not even the asthma could touch it.

Lying on his stomach in the hospital bed, Bub imagined a thick brush, like his mom's wallpaper paste brush, filled with red paint and gently swishing over his body. It started at the heel of his right foot and did one leg at a time, working slowly upward in gentle half-strokes, the numb heat from the paint tingling his skin only where the brush had been. It did his legs, his entire back, then went down to his stomach and started up the front. By the time it got to his chest he was asleep.

-4-
The Ground Blossoms

On Sunday morning, the day before Bub and Spotty planned to quit the band together, they stood beneath the crucifix in their black and white altar boy outfits at Saint Catherine's Holy Catholic Church. As Father Jim asked the parishioners to call to mind their sins, Spotty, with hands folded and profile to the congregation, began to develop an erection—his second one that day. Luckily, his cassock and surplice and stomach rode on his body in such a way as to hide his altar erections from sight, but he was nervous about it anyway, so he used a trick he'd learned almost by accident a few Sundays before—hiking up his cassock, slipping his hand deep in his right pocket, and curling his fingers skyward, thus sliding the erection up and around unnoticed until its underside was held secure by the inside lining of his zipper.

"That's number two for today," Spotty whispered to Bub, as the choir led the congregation in the Glory to God. "I had one when I was lighting the candles—a big one then—and one now."

"You're a sex fiend, Spot," Bub whispered out one side of his mouth.

Spotty and Bub had nearly mastered the art of whispering out the side of the mouth so their fathers wouldn't notice them talking on the altar. It was harder for Bub, because he usually got stuck standing on Spotty's right, which meant he had to use the left side of his mouth—the same side his father could see if he watched real hard. Bub was beginning to be able to say certain words without really moving his lips.

Suddenly everyone stopped singing and Father Jim let out a cough to warn the boys to be silent. He could hear their whisperings well enough to make out a few words, and he had cautioned them before about talking during mass, mostly because their words tended to become giggles, then sputters, then, in Bub's case, outright chokes and violent coughs. Hearing the priest's cough, Bub tensed. He knew that Father Jim might be able to tell if he even *thought* about doing some sins while he was serving on the altar, and he vowed to himself not to talk to Spotty for the rest of the mass.

There was one time, Spotty had warned Bub, that Father Jim had somehow figured out Spotty had been having an erection during mass, and after mass he had taken him into the dark confessional booth, made him pull down his pants, and slapped his hard penis with a cold spoon.

"Did it go down?" Bub had asked, fascinated.

"It got bigger," Spotty had said, rounding out his eyes. "And it stayed bigger too."

But that had been a year before when Bub was only eleven, and he had since ceased to believe the story, and was thinking that maybe Spotty didn't even know what an erection was.

While the choir sang the Responsorial Psalm, Spotty nudged Bub in the side. "Get any hard ones today, Bobby? I think maybe I had one this morning too, when I woke up, and this one's been on for about five minutes already. Five freakin minutes. What time is it?"

"Be quiet," Bub hissed. "I think he can hear us."

"What time is it?" Spotty said, a little louder.

"Twenty after ten."

"Time me," Spotty said.

When the congregation stood up for the Gospel, Bub noticed Father Jim rolling his head a bit to one side, and he felt a piercing glance, almost a burning in his own neck, as if God himself had frowned directly at him. Actually, Father Jim was simply stretching his neck to crack it, limbering up for his Homily about Doubting Thomas. Thomas, the priest had decided to affirm, was perhaps the most intelligent of the apostles. He was an early biologist. He was courageous enough and articulate enough to challenge Christ's resurrection from the dead on the grounds of physical evidence. He wished to probe Christ's side with his own fingers, to peer into his heart with his own microscope. "In short," the priest planned to say in closing, "'Doubting' Thomas was not all thumbs." He was a little concerned that the pun would be lost on his audience. He thought that perhaps wagging both thumbs in the air would be effective.

Just as Father finished the Gospel reading and people settled into the pews, Spotty nudged Bub again. "How many hard ones today? For you. How many?"

"Four and half," Bub said, just to shut him up.

Bub wasn't sure if what he'd been having the last few months could be called true erections, but he kept an approximate count of them, and one day he'd had twelve between breakfast and dinner. Spotty had sworn that it was impossible unless you had a lot of kids, but Bub had not backed down, and Spotty told him that if he had too many in a row he would go completely bald and his fingernails would rot.

During Father's Homily on Thomas, which was sprinkled intermittently with the laughter of both nervous and amiable parishioners, Father Jim kept being distracted by jokes that he might pepper through his Homily the next week. The dwindling view that the Catholic Church was simply a place to "pay, pray, and obey" came to mind, and T. S. Eliot's remark about the church as "rugs, jugs, and candlelight" seemed equally promising, but the priest worried that too much humor might extirpate his meaning. Prudently, he closed his Homily on Thomas with a spontaneous blessing for all the "Doubting Christians" in the world, stretching forth one palm and closing his eyes tightly.

All through the Homily, Spotty and Bub had to sit next to each other on the hard wooden seats that had starshapes cut into them where their butts rested. Sitting in the seats, they faced the congregation directly, and Father Jim's Homilies lasted about ten minutes, so real conversation was extremely difficult. Nevertheless, Spotty kept nudging Bub secretly, reporting on his erection's progress and asking what time it was, hissing that he was going to set a new record. Actually, his erection had gone down after about two minutes.

Later in the mass, when the boys were putting the little cruets of water and wine down on the table where the priest couldn't detect their whispering for a few moments, conversation was much easier.

"Thirty-two minutes," Spotty said to Bub as he picked up the towel Father Jim would soon use to dry his hands. "A new freakin world record."

"You're going to hell for sure," Bub whispered back, a hint of awe in his voice.

Bub thought a lot about hell while he was in church, and most of the time he was convinced that both he and Spotty would indeed be going there someday. Father Jim had told them in catechism class that hell was reserved only for those with the really terrible sins, but Bub figured that an altar boy's sins had to be bigger than most people's because everyone could see you right up there on the altar, and he seemed to think up his most terrible sins exclusively during the mass. He believed that if Father Jim committed even a small sin he would have to go to hell for certain, because, as the town's only priest, he was responsible for the sins of every soul in Hilton all at once, so if he slipped up and died he took everybody's sins with him and spent the rest of eternity doing penance. Or, even worse, Bub thought, maybe they all ended up in purgatory together—all the sinning priests and sinning altar boys, and they had to keep marching through an endless mass in a huge church that nobody came to, all the sinning priests preaching together and all the sinning altar boys forced to stand up the whole time, with none of the boys allowed to say a word to each other until they finally reached eternity or somehow lucked their way out of purgatory and into heaven. The only thing he could figure out about purgatory for certain was that it was just a little bit cold.

While Father Jim broke the big host into pieces he thought about how brittle Christ's bones must have been by the time the spikes were pounded through his feet, and the congregation put up their kneelers, readying themselves to begin the slow shuffle up to the altar for Communion. Meanwhile, Bub's mind started carrying out its favorite sin, which he returned to almost every week. He pretended that he had a gun in his pocket which fired a thin bullet—a deadly accurate, unexploding, placebo-bullet that strictly obeyed all the grass-roots laws of geometry. It didn't go through things but ricocheted neatly rubberlike off them, gradually working its way towards the thing he was secretly aiming for. He imagined that each item hit produced an appropriate sound as the bullet bounced off—a clear ping from the top of the Virgin Mary's statue's head; a muffled thunk from the wooden beams or the altar or the podium from where the gospel was read; a thick bong from the tall brass flowerholders on either side of the altar; a hollow rap from any of the glossy white walls or the curved ceiling which took up a major portion of the space within his firing range—but nothing ever broke and no one ever got hurt, so Bub could shoot it off week after week with no one the wiser. Sometimes he meant the bullet to eventually run into Father Jim, but he never quite had the guts to let it come too close to the crucifix hanging above him, thinking that Jesus himself might come right down and hold up the gun in his pocket for everyone to see if he dared to hit the crucifix. In Bub's mind, the bullet left a solid white jetstream behind itself, forming masses of complicated, overlapping lines all over the church, and it almost always petered out before actually hitting its target.

On this day, while Bub waited for the priest to hand the cups of wafers and wine around to the Eucharistic ministers, the bullet was eventually headed over to the tall red box, where the collection money was dumped and guarded between two sets of steel teeth, but the bullet's path was abruptly halted when Bub had to stand up and follow Spotty down to the aisle where the people were filing up for Communion.

Bub's job was to stand next to Father Jim and hold the round gold plate under the host as it was pulled from the cup and laid on somebody's outstretched tongue or in the cradle of their cupped hands. His plate actually spent little time exactly under the host during its movement, because usually he couldn't tell if the person was going to use his hands or his mouth until it was almost too late. Some people switched from week to week, or worse, they made a last minute decision. The important body parts were at different elevations and the people were at different heights, and Bub also felt very weird when people opened their mouths like that in front of him—some of the mouths gaping wide and the heads tilted back and even the lips curled up so he could see the gums bulging out, and other mouths, usually the younger ones, just barely open and the little snake-tip of the tongue slipping out only long enough to barely catch the round wafer before it disappeared backwards and out of sight forever. The whole process was so complicated and weird for Bub that he just held the gold plate somewhere near the person's bellybutton most of the time, and stared at their faces to keep track of how many of them kept their eyes closed through the whole strange thing. Father Jim had explained to Bub that the bread was transformed into Christ's actual *body* during the mass, and, as you ate it each week, your own body gradually resembled Christ's body more and more. But Bub wasn't convinced. No matter how many wafers he ate, he looked nothing like the body pinned to the cross above him, and he couldn't help picturing a miniature Christ actually stapled onto a little cross made of matchsticks or toothpicks and lodged somewhere at the bottom of his stomach, upsetting the works with the sharp wooden edges, and the trickles of blood from the wounds coating all the other ugly remnants of food down there. He always made sure to chew his own wafer into the tiniest possible pieces before swallowing.

When Mr. Lilly, who always took the host in his hands, came up, Bub jerked the plate down so he would be sure to have it under his father's hands, and he bumped Father Jim's arm just enough to knock the host down onto his plate. Startled, Bub tipped the plate and watched as the wafer flip-flopped, seemingly in slow motion, down to the floor.

Father Jim carefully bent at the waist, holding the cup up high, and reached down to retrieve the host. Mr. Lilly never took his eyes off his son.

"Dad. Sorry. I didn't see you. I can get another one."

Mr. Lilly hissed at his son to be quiet while Spotty sputtered audibly from somewhere nearby, and the priest carefully laid the retrieved host in Mr. Lilly's still-waiting hands.

"Be sure to consume it," he said quietly.

Mr. Lilly took the host, placed it on his tongue, and headed back down the aisle, his son's appalled eyes never moving from him until he reached his pew, as if Bub believed that God would at any moment come charging right at him out of his father's back, seeking restitution for his sin.

After mass, while Bub and Spotty were extinguishing the candles and Father Jim was in the sacristy, pulling the green robe over his head safely out of hearing distance, Spotty told Bub that now *he* was the one who was surely going to hell.

"Wait till lunch. Mister Math is gonna jam that Communion cracker right down your throat. He didn't eat it; I know he didn't. I saw him put it in his pocket and he's gonna save it till lunch and make you eat it with all the dirt and footprints and stuff all over it and you're gonna choke on it and go straight to freakin hell."

But Bub didn't say anything. He was trying to pinpoint the funny feeling he had going on in his chest. It wasn't asthma; it seemed something like it but was a lot weirder—not because he was worried about what his father would do over lunch, nor because he knew that the little round host was a little fragment of God, perhaps a toenail or an elbow, and he had dumped it right out on the floor as if it was a nickel. What alarmed him was that he had actually sinned BIG with Jesus hanging right behind him, and his father had stared right back at him without blinking and swallowed the wafer down, and Bub's mind, in a panic, had automatically set the bullet off with no particular destination; there was nothing he could do to stop it and no way to know what it might hit, and it must still be out there caroming back and forth off things all on its own. And, on top of it all, Bub thought maybe he had a bit of an erection.

All the way home in the car his father surprised him by not mentioning what had happened at Communion at all, giving Bub the desperate urge to tell somebody about the whole strange mess—about Goldy and the band and the bullet and purgatory and maybe even erections—but he didn't know who. All that his parents talked about in the car was Bub's grandmother.

Bub's grandmother had been in the Hilton Manor for two years with Alzheimer's disease. Two months after her husband died, the police had found her wandering in the woods almost sixty miles from Hilton, where she had hitched a ride from a teenage boy, and Lillian had decided to put her in the home. Every few months one of the doctors at the Manor advised Mrs. Lilly that her mother could pass away at any time, or that she might sink wholly into senile dementia, but she doggedly continued to live on, slipping in and out of timelessness, talking almost incessantly, as though her constant filling of the air with words would resuscitate her nearly obsolete kidneys, and lungs, and heart, and feet.

Today, Lillian's mother—Anna—was aware that it was Sunday and that her daughter would be visiting; despite the naugahyde straps connecting her arms to the bed rails, she had managed to prop herself up in bed and comb her hair. Just after she watched a church service on television, confused by the hit-and-run hymns of the evangelist's choir, the seizure hit.

She had seizures every few weeks. By now Anna knew what the seizure would do to her: her breathing would happen in her throat instead of her chest and the rapid little gasps would shiver down along her arms and legs and then back up to her head, and she would be forced to talk: to tell the room everything she saw, no matter how empty and terrible it all was, not knowing which place she would end up in today—in the bed, on the ceiling, in the television, through the window—but knowing for sure that she was not going to die today, no, she was not going to die, because if she was going to die today all the foolish body-whirling wouldn't be so very real and slippery and stupid.

When the Lillys walked into Anna's room after church, the seizure had just started, and she put all her effort into trying to tell them about it.

"Just put me. Put me. On the ground."

"It's okay mother," Lillian said. "I'm here. Look, Bub came along."

Anna tried to control her words by holding her head still.

"Oh, Lilly. Oh. God. Shit. Out. Oh."

"Hi Gramma," Bub said brightly.

"Oh God. They've got me in big belts."

Lillian squeezed her mother's shoulder tightly so she would know someone was in the room with her. A nurse came in and stood at the foot of the bed, holding a syringe filled with green liquid, saying that Anna hadn't slept the night before and that she was on all the medicine they could give her, and the best thing they could do now was to help her calm down.

"She's having a seizure," Mr. Lilly said. "Get the doctor."

As the woman in the white dress left, Anna felt the bed shaking and remembered she was somewhere in a room. She saw two tall figures turned a little sideways and shimmering next to her, then Bub's face was clearly suspended in front of her, his eyes bulging like a toad's, his mouth flapping open, then closed. Open, then closed. It was her grandson, come to play.

"Bub. Bub. Bub. I. Know. Bub. Blossoms. Get the tree. Stop it. Shit. Put me. Down."

"She's having a seizure," Mrs. Lilly said to the doctor as he glided into the room—he was all whiteness, all calm, fluid motion.

"The tree. Blossoms. On the ground."

"Where are you Mrs. Smith?" the doctor shouted.

"She's dreaming," Bub said.

"Hush," Mrs. Lilly said.

"Oh. God. Oh. Take this shit. Off me."

"She thinks it's spring," Bub said. "With cherry blossoms. On the ground." He could picture it perfectly. "Are you dreaming Gramma?" he shouted.

"Hush Bub," Mrs. Lilly said.

"Yes. Yes. Dreaming. God."

"Do you know where you are Mrs. Smith?" the doctor said.

"It's a dream," Bub said. "She just can't sleep."

Anna was suddenly soothed because Bub was there—staring innocently in her eyes, unafraid and untouchable. He lifted her, cradled her in his arms, and gently lowered her to the ground. Where the blossoms were. He laid her down on the pile of white petals—all softness, all rest.

Then the doctor talked to her, and there were no things in the room but his voice. He asked her how old she was and what day it was and where she had just been. Anna told him she was seventy-one and it was Sunday and that she had just fallen out the window. He hiked up her robe and squeezed her stringy calves a few times, tapped on her knees with a little triangular hammer, then asked her if she knew his name. He gave her two words to remember: "green" and "apple." After two minutes she forgot the words, but remembered the doctor's name.

The doctor led Lillian and John into the hallway, and Bub sat next to his grandmother's bed, nervous and happy. He leaned close to Anna and talked.

"I dropped Communion on the floor today Gramma. Dad had to eat it."

"Bub," she said, reaching out and touching his cheek. "It's terrible. Bub. Stupid."

"I shot off the bullet and he just walked away, and he didn't even say anything about it Gramma, but I sinned."

"Bub," she whispered, leaning closer to him. "You saw it. A tree. And blossoms."

"It was spring," Bub said.

"Yes. We sat. Together. On the ground."

"It was a dream Gramma."

Anna was starting to remember everything. Her daughter fed her dinner at 5:30 every night. Last night was mashed potatoes and string beans. Her son-in-law squeezed her hand so tight that her arm shook. Her grandson never blinked when he looked at her. There was a cherry tree underneath his bedroom window. Green was spelled g-r-e-e-n.

Anna heard her daughter sniffling in the hallway, and there were long pauses after the doctor spoke.

"You're a good boy. Oh. God."

"It was weird, Gramma. And I swore in church. A couple times."

Anna was so tired that she could hardly hear Bub's words anymore, but he looked as if he was about to cry.

"Go to confession," she said.

"I can't." Bub knew it was true. He and Spotty agreed. Bub could never go to confession again, they had decided. He was beyond confession: he was wheezing his way into hell.

"Confess. God will. Save you."

Anna groped for Bub's hand, squeezed it, and told him that she was going to sleep now. He watched her face smooth itself out as she closed her eyes and drifted farther and farther away from his words, and he realized that his grandmother must know how to paint herself to sleep just as he did, and maybe that was where he had first learned it. Maybe she had taught him how to do it a long time ago while he bounced up and down on her couch or dug a hole in her garden. Maybe she was painting herself red or yellow or white right in front of him right now. She had invented it when she was just a little girl.

As her breathing slowed and the room seemed to darken, he pulled the blankets up over his grandmother's chest, so nobody else could see her body as it changed colors for him—so nobody else could know their secret.

-5-
The Talking Screen

As Bub slipped into line for the confessional booth a few hours later, the same mood filled the air as when he sang in the shower—every noise he made had the danger of spilling into something that sounded like a series of snapped twigs, a virulent rolling cackle, a confused commotion that would instantly make people turn their heads if they heard. In his shower at home, the danger ended when Bub turned off the water, but in the church it followed him long after he left the confessional that day—echoing faintly in the background as he rode his bike, or played his trumpet, or revved the engine in his chest, sick for sleep.

Each Saturday and Sunday afternoon in the back of Saint Catherine's church, two confessional booths waited underneath two ghostly white triangles—a little like stout, convex dunce caps—that glowed. Father Jim controlled the glow of the left triangle with a light switch; the other triangle lit when a confessor made contact with the kneeler inside the booth.

Bub stood in line outside the door, watching the triangle blink on and off above him, and watched the people walk back into the shadowy church when the triangle went out for a moment, to kneel and mumble things that he couldn't quite catch, but which sounded remarkably like his father's muffled voice filtering up through the floorboards of his bedroom.

He'd only been to confession once, when he'd made his first confession in the second grade. All he could remember about it was that he had peed his pants, and he knew that peeing your pants in church was a very big sin, so he had never gone again.

Waiting in line, he imagined what the ideal confessional booth would be like inside—a dimly-lit maze of holey wooden walls and sloping floors, with maybe a skeleton or a bat dropping down harmlessly once in awhile. There was a rotten board around one corner and he could fall screaming down into an abyss of almost one-foot deep, to jump out laughing and then wait secretly for Spotty to fall into the hole behind him. Maybe even one of those funhouse mirrors that made your body waggle into distorted blobs and skinny tubes. And Father Jim waiting at the end of the maze to shake his hand and buy him some cotton candy.

Father Jim's visions of the confessional booth were very different. He had the view that the modern confessional needed to be demystified—darkly hushed sin-drops did not reconcile one with God; open grief was the ticket. Although he kept one-third of the confessional booth dark and compartmentalized at the insistence of his parishioners, he hoped for a time when all confessions would be face-to-face or even shared openly with the faithful community. This would allow the priest to be perceived as more than a mumbler of charms or spells and would give the parishioners easier access to the rainwater of mercy—rainwater was his favorite floating metaphor. The confessional booth in which he sat, he thought, was still too much like a sentry box, an airplane toilet, a poorly lit space capsule, a coffin tipped up. Certainly reconciliation with God took place, but not, as far as Father Jim was concerned, in the most purging of environments.

When Bub entered the confessional booth, he found it was a high wooden box lit by a pink nightlight, with a wide padded rail—a kneeler—running along one wall, and a stiff square screen, like a window screen, in the middle of the wall above the kneeler.

The screen talked.

Fascinated, Bub stepped up onto the kneeler, which set the triangle outside his door glowing, and tentatively touched one corner of the talking screen with his index finger, wishing that it would reveal a secret doorway.

It talked again.

Then he saw a fragmented version of Father Jim's face fuzzily moving around just a few inches away behind the screen, the nose and chin darker blotches than the rest, and the forehead overly shiny. The hair was just a few connected black boxes. Bub couldn't make out the eyes at all, but there were two oblong areas of seeming vacancy, and he knew it was Father Jim because he recognized the smell. Except when he smelled like burning incense or sweat, the priest smelled distantly of mint toothpaste.

Bub sat down sideways on the kneeler and began flicking the pink nightlight on and off with his finger. He wasn't sure what to say; he didn't feel like confessing now that it was all so stifling and unimaginative. He wanted a nightlight for his own room.

"May God be in your heart and in your mind so that you may make a sincere confession, in the name of the Father, the Son, and the Holy Spirit."

Bub said nothing, but could feel the priest's expectation brimming over in the little booth.

"Are you there?" Father Jim's voice said.

Bub flicked off the nightlight and stood on the kneeler, both hands pressed against the screen. All the priest could see of him was an imprint of two small hands fanned out a foot from his face.

"Hi," said Bub, his voice feeling strangely powerful in the dark.

"All right. Begin."

Five years before, in training for first confession, Bub had had to compose a list of his sins and read it off in front of the whole catechism class. His list had admitted to deceit, messiness, minor sloth, open annoyance, and the dream of running away from home, but his life had gotten much more complicated now, and he had no list to rely on. He remembered a trick that Spotty had mentioned though: to make up at least five small sins really fast in case you got stuck, but secretly think inside about your real sins when you said them, and the priest would give you your penance and let you go home unscathed. Bub would resort to this if he had to.

"I didn't throw my trumpet in the pond."

"Pardon me?"

"I didn't do it. But I pretended I did it and I saw it sink to the bottom in my head. It got all black water up into the tubes and all, and the only way to get it back is to dive down and pick it up, and you couldn't play it anyway. All the water would run out."

"Did you lie to your parents about it?" Father Jim said. He realized during the speech that it was Bub. He didn't remember Bub ever coming to him for confession before.

"No, I didn't tell them all of it." His voice felt thinner now.

"Are you sorry for it?"

"Yes. Definitely."

"Good. What else?"

Nervous, Bub jumped back and forth from the kneeler to the floor, unknowingly clicking the glowing triangle above his door off, then on, off, then on.

"I got asthma again. Four times in two days. When I get it I sneak down in the middle of the night. I eat a bunch of Raisin Bran, then I crumble up some other raisins from the real raisin box and some Corn Flakes and mix 'em all up in the Raisin Bran box. So nobody will know. If it's really bad I get up on a chair and open the freezer and breathe in it cold for a long time. The air in there is a lot better. Really clean. But I only breathe it until the asthma goes away, and I didn't tell mom. I think she'd get mad."

By the tugging inside his pants, Bub knew then that he had to pee. He fluttered his arms around a bit and hopped back and forth—an odd but impressive imitation of a hungry baby sparrow, begging to be fed. The two people in the line outside the door could see the triangle blinking on and off and hear Bub hopping around inside, but they waited their turns, reverently refusing to meet each other's eyes. Bub reached down and squeezed his penis area between his fingers, holding back the urine with the pressure.

"It's okay," Father Jim said. "Now slow down. Why don't we have face-to-face confession, Bub."

The fuzzy boxes of the priest's body disappeared from behind the screen and stepped around to the back of Bub's booth, sliding open the purple velvet curtain and magically revealing two chairs. Bub walked in, entranced. The chair seats were bright green bulgy squares of fabric that lay in a warm inviting grid. The priest sat down on one chair and motioned Bub to the other one.

"Hey, it's a curtain. Like at the circus. I thought it was a wall."

"It's all right. Now sit down and we'll finish."

"I can see you now."

"Yes. Go ahead and sit down. I picked these chairs out myself. How long since your last confession?"

"I can't remember," Bub lied.

Father Jim didn't believe him, but felt suddenly delighted by Bub's presence. He was actually a charming boy, the priest thought, with the unparted hair and round, unwrinkled face that you found on thousands of boys his age. That face might appear suddenly on any bottle of medicine or any cereal box. The thing that made him really different was the asthma. This confession was the most interesting one he'd had all day.

"What sins can you remember, besides the trumpet and the asthma, that you haven't told me about yet?"

Bub sat down. He didn't have to pee anymore. It was strange to be looking directly at Father Jim's face. He was used to staring up at him over his chest, fascinated by all the nose hair. Now the face was lit only on one side and the nose seemed to have disappeared completely. He could make out little cracks in the lips and noticed, for the first time, that the hair on the priest's sideburns was actually curly. He also appeared to have hair growing out of his ears. The gray, fragmented light reminded Bub of the way things looked in the hospital at night.

"I lied. A lot. And I dropped the Communion in church. My dad ate it. I swore. A couple of times. And I quit the band."

"Is it a sin to quit the band?"

"No. I lied. I didn't quit. I just want to."

"Okay. How are you doing right now? Is anything wrong?" Father Jim knew that Bub was an emotionally intense boy, and that he and Spotty were in the band together. Maybe the two boys had had a fight on the altar that morning. That could be what he'd overheard whispered pieces of, and perhaps that was what was behind all the meandering sin-blurbs that Bub was coming up with.

"My gramma died," Bub said. "Well she didn't really die—she's okay. But I think she's gonna die. Soon. She told me to come to confession, so I came."

"It's good that you came. You're being very truthful. Are you sorry for your sins?"

"Yes," Bub said, "and that's all."

Father Jim bowed his head and prayed spontaneously for a few moments while Bub stared at the top of half his head. He thanked God for bringing Bub to confession; he prayed for the boy's good health and peace of mind; he hoped that Bub might interrupt him to talk some more. Then the priest talked Bub through his Act of Contrition, assured him that this confession had cleansed his body and soul of those sins remembered and not remembered, and told him that he would be praying for Bub's grandmother. For his penance, Bub was supposed to say ten Hail Marys and two Our Fathers, and when he got home he was supposed to tell his mother that he'd been eating the Raisin Bran at night. He decided not to say anything about the Raisin Bran, and he couldn't remember all the words to the Hail Mary, but after leaving the confessional he knelt at one of the front pews and said a bunch of Our Fathers absently, all the while unable to think about anything but all the real sins that he had failed to confess to Father Jim. Ripping off cupcakes from K-Mart with Spotty. Spitting on the floor at school, and once on the back of a teacher's high heel by accident. Lying during confession on purpose, and then forgetting how many prayers he was supposed to say. Skipping confession for years and telling his parents he was going, while he really sat in his secret place in the woods, hoping for a thunderstorm. Stamping great big dirty words into the snow last winter with Spotty, that you could see from really high up in an airplane and, he just realized, probably from heaven too. Setting off the bullet right into the organist's belly. Making loud noises on purpose while his father slept on the couch. And erections. Countless erections, or things that were like erections, and not just in church, but on the bike, in the car, in school, and twice at dinner.

Bub thought over all his sins as he knelt at the pew and wondered if God could kill him right then and there, while Father Jim finished up with the other two confessors. Then Father clicked off his triangle and went around the church closing the windows and turning off the lights soundlessly, until he glided up to where Bub knelt in the darkened church, sniffling just a little with his head down.

"You're certainly doing a lot of praying today, aren't you Bub."

They were alone in the church together.

"I have erections," Bub blurted out.

His chest gurgled a bit, threatening to start chugging, but his ears were much more alarming. A strange hum kicked around in them, forcing him to look around, startled, and forget all about Father Jim for a moment, while all the statues simultaneously turned their heads to look at him. There was the Virgin Mary, peeking over her blue shoulder and closing her eyes knowingly, and Joseph, wincing the way his father did when he practiced the trumpet. The tall brown saint with the rope around his waist didn't seem to move at all, but Bub swore that he made a little sound, like a chuckle. Then the hum stopped and he looked up at Father Jim, who had his hand on Bub's shoulder.

"What do you think about when you have erections?"

"My bike. Nothing. I don't know."

"It's okay." The priest was happy. Here was a boy convinced of his guilt, but unable to name the thing which troubled him. Here was youth, fresh and green.

"I almost had one when I said the Our Father."

"It's all right," Father Jim said. "It's perfectly natural. It means that you're healthy. God forgives you."

Bub wondered if God had erections, and realized that it must be an incredible sin even to think about it.

"Do you need a ride home?"

"No, I have my bike," he said, standing up and wiping his face. "Thanks."

"Talk to your father about it. And don't worry. They won't hurt you."

Bub walked out of the church, hearing the heavy metal side door suck shut behind him, and ran to his bike, feeling that he could float if he wanted. Now tomorrow he would quit the band

and tell Mr. Bailey and Spotty and maybe even his mom that he'd been to confession and the priest had looked right at him and said that he didn't have to play the trumpet at all. He could glide up and down like a bird if he wanted—dash around like a finch, darting from bush to bush. He was free.

All the way home on his bike he had an erection, he was sure, that was larger than his thumb.

RADIATOR DREAMS

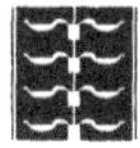

Mrs. Bill's son, Jerry, usually watched her tend her garden for hours from his invention room window just to be certain that she was indeed insane. Although Mrs. Bill boasted an entire hardware story of non-mechanical gardening tools in her garage, Jerry noted that she had a fetish for a particular shovel. Sometimes she even stood just below his window, embracing the shovel in her calloused hands and, Jerry was sure, whispered intimacies to it. Then Jerry opened his window and glided his torso out over his mother's head, with his abdomen and palms on the windowsill, his knees locked, his shoes hooked into holes he had beat into the dusty, hardwood floor with a croquet mallet, a puttyknife, and an awl. Then he could see that her face was raised to the great shovel god, her lips trembling in maniacal adoration. At just the right moment, when Mrs. Bill was entirely entranced, Jerry imagined himself clubbing her with a zucchini, wrestling the shovel from her, and smashing her again and again over the head until she drifted off into apoplexy and couldn't tend her garden anymore. Jerry was twenty-four years old.

Mrs. Bill's full name was Eddiah Joan Bill, but all her friends, and Jerry, called her Edda. She embodied a special kinship with the vegetable kingdom. She resented all machines because, as she said, "machines are an insult to the bounty of the earth." She flatly refused to buy a power lawn mower. "Nothing powered by gasoline," she insisted, "can outdo the heart of a weed." Then she chuckled.

But Mrs. Bill was a practical woman. She realized that machines, like people, had their roles to fulfill, and sometimes you had to hire someone to drag them through your soil. "All I ask," she would say to the tillerman, "is that you till my garden with love." When plowing, the tillerman kept his balance by turning his green baseball cap to the left side and his pink tongue to the right.

For months Jerry, the inventor, had been plotting to trick his mother into buying a riding lawn mower. "To make it easier on yourself," he told her with a secret smile. Actually he liked to imagine her shrieking figure reeling along uncontrollably on the machine with the throttle stuck, churning up all her vegetables, or randomly slamming her into a tree. Maybe a nice hole in the earth would open up and suck her away, Jerry hoped. At breakfast one morning, he thought she was about primed to purchase the mower.

"But the blades on that handmower are so old," Jerry said.

Mrs. Bill noisily chomped on a carrot with her false teeth.

"For your health, Edda," he said, gently flicking his fingers over her wrist. "So you don't have to push around that old manual mowing machine anymore."

"It is not," she said, squeezing an acorn squash in her fist, "a machine."

And that had been that. That had always been that. Mrs. Bill shook a clenched iron fist against all machines. When Jerry had bought a TV, Mrs. Bill smashed an eggplant all over the screen. Then she wrote up some guidelines and posted them in the parlor room.

THESE RULES SHALL GOVERN THIS HOUSE, JERRY

1.) You may invent anything you wish, but none of your inventions may be machines.
2.) A machine is any mechanical or senselessly noisy item used to annoy another person, such as a radio, jackhammer, or can opener.
3.) Although your red wagon is in some ways a machine, it is allowed so you can haul parts for your inventions.
4.) Two wrong machines don't make a right machine.

This, she knew, would offer the boy direction and incentive to keep making inventions which were not machines.

"Ever since he was a child," Edda was fond of saying, "I knew Gerald would be an inventor. He was always having bright ideas. Just like a light bulb. And dreams. Dreams you couldn't imagine."

Actually Jerry had never invented anything, but he had written to the government several times requesting patents. Since he got no replies, Edda assured everyone that the government was keeping its eye on Jerry, just waiting for the perfect moment to issue the winning patent. Actually Mrs. Bill didn't think Jerry would ever really win a patent, but she had to keep up appearances for his sake. Actually Jerry never sent any of the letters he showed to his mother. He kept them locked away in a folder in his invention room marked "Letters Not Sent." It was all part of a psychological game he was playing with Mrs. Bill without her knowing it. He even told her about his inventions in severe detail, but never let her see them because they were in the "nominal stage." She didn't know what that meant, but it sounded like something an inventor would say. Jerry recorded each instance of her repeating "nominal stage" on a bar graph in a brown folder. One day she said it fourteen times.

Mrs. Bill was especially proud that none of Jerry's inventions would be machines. She told everyone who listened that Jerry's inventions didn't depend on electricity or gasoline or extension cords or tubes or disgusting buttons or pumps or sharp gray metal or any other contraptions: they were completely independent, just like him. Of course she couldn't tell people too much about the inventions, or they might steal Jerry's ideas. She told them that someone's ideas might be stolen if they were not yet patented.

Although Mrs. Bill was talkative and charitable with her friends in this manner, she did not really like any of them. She reasoned logically that her disposition was more suited to gardening than to liking people. So she worked on both at once. Each new year she counted all those who claimed to be her enemies, and some she considered her enemies instinctively, and planted that same number of cabbage seeds. She planted an extra dozen just in case. Whenever she felt particularly hateful, she gazed over her cabbage plants like a great vegetable goddess, holding aloft her shovel, and visualized the heads of her enemies poking up out of the leaves. When she could imagine all of their faces clearly, gazing upward in neat, submissive rows with their mouths open, she prayed for them. Each one individually. All of her enemies' faces were green.

She prayed things like "help so-and-so in the ways listed in my head," or "help so-and-so to be a better so-and-so," or even "help this cabbage head to grow." Of course, she was really praying for her enemies and her cabbages at the same time. She was killing two birds with one stone.

When she ran out of enemies and cabbages to pray for, she stood under Jerry's window and prayed for his inventions.

"Dear Jesus," she prayed, "help Gerald's latest invention to be a smashing success for us, and help him to know You as a real, talkable, everyday person like me—"

She was in just such a state of prayer one Saturday morning, and Jerry was watching over her from his invention room window. Her lips nearly kissed the shovel this time, and Jerry was sure he could make out either the word "Jesus" or "Jerry" or "Jingle." He pictured her then with a cucumber in each ear. A tomato in her mouth. Cauliflower sprang up between her absurd toes. A parsley sprig was lodged under a dirty, cracked fingernail. She had stopped wearing fingernail polish years ago. She certainly looked like a damned idiot, Jerry thought. Then he ran to get the front door before she heard the unexpected knock.

Gulliver Pulver stood before Jerry in the parlor room doorway holding a free newspaper. He had been nurtured on Gerber strained apricot baby food until he was four. Then his mother, on an obstetrician's advice, had switched him to Quaker oatmeal. His chest fell in one smooth, pink roll down to his thighs, and the fat around his knees commingled when he managed to stand still. He had a tiny saliva bubble on his lips from breathing so heavily, because he had just ridden his banana bike all the way up the hill. The bubble fell from his lips and splattered on the linoleum of the parlor room floor. Gulliver was eleven years old.

"And what's your name?" Jerry said, quick as a cat.

"Gull . . . Gulliver. Gulliver Pulver," Gulliver stuttered,

confused. The newspaper office had said that a Mrs. Bill lived at this address. This was not a Mrs. Bill. The man had traces of whisker on his oval, concave face. From the neck up he looked like a cake of Camay with a rash.

"So little Gully," Jerry said, "what do you want?"

"Are you Mr. Bill?"

"No," Jerry said, annoyed. "He's dead. Mrs. Bill killed him. Call me Jerry."

"Yes . . . um . . . is Mrs. Bill here?"

"Oh," Jerry said, "she's off foddering around in the garden."

The screen door to the kitchen opened, and Jerry hushed Gulliver. Behind the wall, they could hear Mrs. Bill's body rumbling towards the parlor room, floor boards groaning under her weight. Gulliver's eyes popped wide when she entered the parlor room. He dropped the newspaper.

"Try not to laugh at her," Jerry whispered quickly.

"Gerald," she accused him, "is this another one of your little friends?"

"Why no, Edda," Jerry said sweetly. "This is Gulliver Pulver, and he's here to see you."

"And what can I do for you, Mr. Pulver?" she demanded, getting right to the point. She always called small boys Miss-ter to let them know she was in charge. She stood before Gulliver like a huge, red tractor, sputtering wisps of steam, clay on her boots, shorts tight around her knees, stomach bulging and hard, her shovel poised on her shoulder like a club, dripping mud. Her square nose was flanked by two pierogie-shaped cheeks—rolling mountains she managed to crest only by forcing her eyeballs to the tops of their sockets as she stared down at Gulliver, getting to the point.

"I'm sellin' special 'scription rates, ma'am. I represent *The Daily Chronicle*, a local newspaper with current 'formation." Like any good businessman, he had memorized a speech, Mrs. Bill noted with approval.

Edda was satisfied that she had sufficiently intimidated the boy and decided to be friendly.

She slapped her meaty hand down on his shoulder. "Well then Mr. Pulver, let's talk business. Gerald, fetch Mr. Pulver a nice little sugar cookie and half a glass of milk."

By the time Jerry had returned from the kitchen with Gully's snack, Mrs. Bill had locked up the whole deal. Gulliver would deliver *The Daily Chronicle* promptly without fail Monday through Saturday by 6:00 p.m. sharp until Mrs. Bill otherwise terminated their agreement, and he would collect his set fee each Saturday morning, notifying her one month in advance if set fee was scheduled to increase. Gulliver gave Mrs. Bill an official white and black *Chronicle* card from which he would punch holes weekly as a receipt with Mrs. Bill witnessing, and Jerry hung the card on a bare nail in the paneling by the parlor room door.

After closing the deal, Mrs. Bill told Jerry to show Gulliver to the parlor room door and rumbled back to her garden.

"Mrs. Bill said that you're an inventor, Mr. Bill," the boy said.

"Call me Jerry. I'm really a magician, Gully," Jerry whispered confidentially.

"But she said you're an inventor," Gully said.

"That's part of my magic, Gully," Jerry winked. "She thinks I'm an inventor because I tricked her into it, but I'm really a magician." Jerry had already instinctively decided to take the boy into his confidence.

"Will you show me a magic trick?" Gully asked.

"Yes Gully, next week, my little Gully," Jerry promised smoothly.

Gully wiggled happily. This had certainly been an exciting day for him. First a new customer and now a magician. "See you next week, Mr. Bill!" he said, struggling onto his banana bike.

"Call me Jerry," Jerry said.

Jerry spent all week in his invention room inventing a magic trick to play on Gully. He had never worked on any of his other inventions quite so zealously. It took him four nails and thirteen needles to get it just right. He had to walk into town to find masonry nails strong enough for the vital incision. Pounding the nails masterfully with an ordinary hammer, he formed a tiny but perfectly round incision halfway into the top edge of a 1930 peace dollar coin, then cleaned out the incision scrupulously with a sliver of 120-grit sandpaper wrapped around a toothpick. Then he lodged the end of a needle into a small vice secured to an orange crate, and chopped off the top and eye of the needle with a small hammer and intentional suddenness. Twelve of the needles he broke were too long or too short, but the last one was just right. He dipped the newly flattened end of the needle carefully into a bowl of Elmer's glue, then forced the glued end of the needle into the incision in the coin with his water-pump pliers, careful not to impair the natural point of the needle by squeezing too indiscriminately. It took him five attempts to get the needle to stay in place, and after each try he had to sandpaper the incision out again and redip the needle. He finally got it secured by holding it perfectly still in place for five minutes while the glue dried. A vein in his left wrist turned purple from the pressure. On the first try, he burnt the end of the needle with the blue tip of a match flame so it blended in better with the color of the coin. Mrs. Bill could hear him whooping away with joy in his invention room all week, and she spent an extra five minutes a day under his window, praying that his new invention would be something useful and completely unlike a machine. Jerry was so involved in his current project that he hardly had time to observe her.

He waited for Gully on the front porch on Saturday morning so he would get to him before Mrs. Bill. It excited him that he could employ something as small and innocent-looking as a trick coin, hidden in an ordinary shirt pocket, in the general scheme against his mother.

As he rode up in front of the house, Gulliver waved to Jerry with one arm and ran his banana bike into a juniper bush on the front lawn. He wrestled the bike out of the bush, then puffed his way up to the porch.

"Will you show me the trick now, Jerry?" he piped.

It was just as he had guessed. Gully's little mind had been absorbed by the trick all week too. He noted also that Gully had called him Jerry. They understood each other now. They were brothers now. They were co-conspirators. They were friends.

"I'll show you," he said, "but only if you promise to do something for me."

Gully gulped.

"After you finish your collecting today, come back here and take a ride into town with me to a curio shop."

He knew that Mrs. Bill took a walking tour every Saturday afternoon and it would be a safe time to plot alone with Gully. Mrs. Bill would never expect anything underhanded could happen during her walking tour.

"What's a curio shop?" Gully asked, a bead of perspiration shooting down his nose, off his chin, under his collar, and into his navel, where it was absorbed by a fuzzball.

"Oh, they have trick chairs and explosives, red snake skins and green popcorn, giant blue marbles, and lots of other items useful for magic tricks," Jerry said with pretended nonchalance.

"You mean a *junk* shop?"

"No Gully, I mean Coco Bunner's Curio Shop!"

"Yeah!" said Gully, his stomach quivering with delight.

So it was all set up. Jerry asked him if his parents would miss him, and Gully assured him that they would not, as long as he was home before dinner. The perfect situation. Jerry warned him not to tell his parents or Mrs. Bill or any other adult, because they certainly wouldn't approve of a boy his age dabbling in magic.

"But what about the trick!" Gully remembered in all the excitement.

"Ah yes Gully, the trick," said Jerry dramatically. "Here we have an ordinary trick coin." He instantly produced the peace dollar coin with the burnt needle hook from his shirt pocket, and held it at a safe distance from Gully at eye level between the index and little fingers of his right hand, just as he had practiced.

"Watch this coin carefully, Gully, very carefully, carefully," he said in a mesmerizing voice. He turned his left side to Gully and made several arc-like passes with the coin from his right hip to the level of his right shoulder, extending his arm fully and holding the coin just at the tips of his fingers. He repeated "carefully, carefully," with each pass. Then when Gully's attention lingered away from Jerry's hip for a moment, Jerry neatly hooked the coin on his pants and pulled his empty hand away. He wore his black corduroys just for the occasion.

Gully was agog. His little mouth was frozen in an O just large enough to stuff a tangerine into, Jerry thought. Or a kiwi. Or a small Macintosh apple. Jerry had him in his grip now, he was sure. He shook his right hand in the air hypnotically and wiggled every finger to prove that the coin was no longer there. He opened and closed his empty fist at varying speeds, while Gully stared on, awestruck. Then he began his methodic handpasses again, repeating "watch carefully, carefully—" At just the right instant he snatched the coin into his hand again, and Gully closed his little mouth and fluttered his hands in front of it in unspeakable admiration. Gully pleaded with him to do it again, but Jerry remarked that a good magician never repeated his tricks, and sent him out to the garden to collect his money from Mrs. Bill.

"I'll be back in a few hours to go to the curio shop!" Gully yelled as he rounded the house.

"It's a date, Gully," Jerry said.

From his invention room window, he watched his mother counting out the coins for Gully while standing among the future turnips. He covered his mouth and chuckled through his nose, thinking how Gully would try to mimic his trick while riding his banana bike home and would make some of the coins disappear, thereby coming up short when he counted his collection money. But he liked Gully. Gully was his little sibling. His thoughts returned darkly to his mother. She was not worthy of tying Gully's sneakers. He called her a mushmelon. A rotted yellow pepper. An onion. He imagined himself breaking her shovel viciously over his knee, while Mrs. Bill was tied to a nearby tree by his little, whooping, painted helper Gully.

Coco Bunner's Curio Shop was the best junkshop in the county. "A shop," Coco told his customers, "where dreams can be bought and sold." He did so much business that he had won a petition for a traffic light at the intersection in front of his shop. Coco didn't just take any junk, he selected what to buy or trade depending on the type of junk in greatest demand on the market. He had sixteen years experience and toured junkshops all over the state once a month, bartering with other junkmen like a prosecuting attorney. On sight he tagged any piece of junk in his mind with an appropriate label: Celebrity Junk, Eccentric Junk, Closet Junk, Attic Junk, Living Room Junk, Mechanical Junk, or Junkity Junk. He also tagged each of his customers by the looks on their faces when they came in the front door: Trendy, Glitsy, Browsy, Ritzy, and Patsy. He had an overabundance of Celebrity Junk this month, and was right in the middle of a special prayer for a Patsy, when Jerry and Gully came bursting through the door. He rang the cowbell next to his cash register merrily.

"Hi, Ho!" yelled Coco. This was his traditional greeting reserved for a Patsy.

"Whaddaya know!" yelled Jerry. This was his traditional greeting reserved for someone he thought knew nothing.

While Coco and Jerry exchanged a slick patter of talk like two expert chess players, Coco took down a blunderbuss from the wall behind him and polished the walnut stock suggestively with Lemon Pledge and a diaper. The doughboy, Coco noted, was sufficiently impressed. Gully rolled his eyes up and down the cluttered shop walls, then began scouring the ceiling, expecting to see more curio hanging there.

"And what does this little marshmallow want?" Coco said suddenly, rumpling Gully's hair. "A glass rose for his mama maybe?" Coco pulled a plastic-stemmed rose with glass petals from a bowling alley display case and rotated it in front of Gully's face. When you shook the rose it snowed inside the petals. A very popular item at Christmas.

"Whoa now, Coco, this boy here is a caution," Jerry said. "I warn you he's one smooth peach. He's liable to just take over your business someday." Jerry patted Gully between the shoulderblades and told him to look around the shop while he talked business.

Jerry had already planned what he would need for his next trick: a strong rope and a heavy object between fifty and seventy-five pounds. But he understood the mechanics of barter. To get a decent price he had to let Coco make his pitch. Coco tried to sell him a box of original Campbell's ketchup bottles and a huge stack of *National Enquirer* magazines; but Jerry already had several stacks of *Star* magazines and he was an inventor, not a collector. He toyed with Coco for a few minutes, then casually let his eye drift to a thick rope stretching from the ceiling to the floor.

"This," Coco said, catching Jerry's eye, "is one reliable rope. It was used on the last man to be hanged in this state by the three Ks." This was the story that another dealer had given to Coco, and although Coco didn't believe it, it instantly turned the rope into Celebrity Junk. The rope was loosening in a few places, so Coco had tied it around a hoof-shaped hook in the ceiling, then stretched it taut and tied the other end of the rope around an old radiator lying on the floor. This stretched the rope sufficiently so that the strands looked a bit tighter.

"Hmmmmmn," said Jerry tentatively. "Well now. Hmmmmmn. What's *this* musty old thing?" he said, pushing at the radiator lying at his foot.

"Ahhhhhhh," said Coco suavely. "Now this radiator was handled by Mr. James Cash Penney hisself! Back before he changed his name to J. C. and opened all those stores."

Jerry placed his chin between the thumb and index finger of his right hand, rested his right elbow in the palm of his left hand, and assumed a skeptical look. He bent down and ran his fingers over the radiator. It was smooth, metallic, and cold, like the edge of a blunt sword. On the bottom the words GOLDEN RULE bumped out harsh and green from the surface. Jerry noted the name on it, stood up, and rubbed the dust from his hands with a disgusted finality, informing Coco that he was no fool, and this was certainly no James Cash Penney radiator.

Coco was ready for him. He plucked the book, *Fifty Years with the Golden Rule*, by James Cash Penney, from the shelf behind him, ceremoniously blew the dust off the cover, and handed it to Jerry. Jerry paged through the book for a moment and the words GOLDEN RULE leapt out magically from almost every page. Impressed, he handed it back and admitted that he might be interested in both the rope and the radiator, for the right price. Coco, who knew a Patsy when he found one, then tried to interest Jerry in a wooden helicopter blade. It was the same blade, said Coco, that the photographer bought in the movie *Blow-Up*, but Jerry wasn't buying it. He also flatly refused the dented trash can that Coco promised had been inhabited by Cookie for the first nine episodes of *Sesame Street*, before Oscar the Grouch moved in on his territory. Finally, they dragged the GOLDEN RULE radiator over to a penny-for-your-weight-and-fortune scale, and it weighed sixty pounds. Perfect. In the end Jerry traded a three-headed brass lamp and seventy-five dollars for the rope and the radiator, and both men shook hands satisfied they had made a shrewd deal.

"Come on, Gully," Jerry said, "before they arrest us for stealing." Gully had been in a corner looking through a magnifying glass larger than his head. Taped on the rim of the glass was a note: "Used by Sherlock Holmes HISSELF!! (-Coco)."

As they pulled the radiator and rope home in the red wagon, Gully pestered Jerry to show him a new trick.

"Patience, Gully," he said. "The first thing a magician learns is patience."

Gully squirmed around on the sidewalk practicing patience. He was beginning to be demanding, Jerry could see that, and coin tricks would not continue to satisfy the boy's curiosity. Eventually Gully would get older. Or worse yet, he would figure out the trick for himself. But Jerry was ready. He had already searched the dictionary for hours as part of his new scheme to occupy Gully's mind profitably.

Once the triple-K rope and the GOLDEN RULE radiator were belted onto a dolly and safely deposited on the porch, Jerry launched his new plan on Gully. He would make Gully a research helper for his next trick. Of course he couldn't reveal what the trick would be because that would spoil the surprise. But Gully could help him do research, and even interpret the research in his own Gully way. He gave him four words to look up for the next trick: gravity, muzzle, browbeat, and torpid. Gully wrote down the words carefully, spelling them gravyt, musle, brallbeat, and torepeed. Then Jerry dismissed him and lugged the rope and radiator up to his invention room, with the unknowing Mrs. Bill still out enjoying her walking tour. Jerry wrote down the first four words Gully was to look up, then stored them in a folder marked "Words On His Mind."

For the next two weeks Jerry worked diligently on his new trick. He measured exact distances, did precise calculations, weighed and reweighed specific objects on the bathroom scale in his invention room, and even built a working model out of toothpicks, thread, a four-penny nail, and clay. The model failed again and again because the thread kept breaking, then Jerry had a bright idea. He held several strands of thread together by the ends in both hands, dropped all but the ends of the threads in a pan of glue, then twisted them together fiercely and pulled outward just hard enough but not too hard until the glue dried. He tied one end of this reinforced thread to a perfectly molded mound of clay, and the other end to the fourpenny nail lodged in a makeshift door formed out of several overlapping rows of toothpicks glued together. The nail served as a doorknob, but of course could not be turned without actually breaking the door. The trick model worked three times in a row, with the edge of a picnic bench representing the windowsill, the toothpick door splattering all over the floor each time. By Friday, Jerry was so exhausted from the excitement that he put aside the trick model and spent much of the day watching over his mother from his invention room window.

Mrs. Bill spent much of Friday praying under Jerry's invention room window. She had heard Jerry pounding away for weeks. He had never been so preoccupied with an invention, and he would give her no details about it. She assured him again and again that, even though the new invention was in the nominal stage, it would be the Patented Big One. He agreed. She prayed for the complete success of his invention, and, since her growing season was just beginning, she prayed for all of her recently planted vegetables. This was a particularly spiritual season of the year for her. She was offering a special litany for her asparagus this year.

That evening Jerry and Mrs. Bill had a conversation.

"I think," began Mrs. Bill, "that our Mr. Pulver has had quite enough time to prove himself, don't you think?"

Jerry could feel his heart pounding in the backs of his knees.

"It has been one month now, and *The Daily Chronicle* has arrived late FOUR times. And from what I hear," she said pointedly, "Mr. Pulver spends far too much time here during his collection rounds."

"But," said Jerry, "you know how boys are, he's just easily distracted. He doesn't realize what's really going on in the world." His throat felt lemony.

"Yes Gerald," agreed Mrs. Bill, "I know how boys are." She had heard from a somewhat reliable neighbor that Mr. Pulver and Gerald spent an inordinate amount of time talking on the front porch together while she prayed in the garden for Gerald's inventions. She had also heard that weeks ago they had returned from somewhere together with a threatening, dark, machine-like object in Gerald's red wagon, and the boy had ridden off on his bike with what looked like an unpaid bill clenched in his little fist. That was all Mrs. Bill needed, for her son and a playmate to be off frolicking somewhere running up unpaid bills for machines when she spent so much time praying for her son's inventions! If there was one thing she wouldn't stand for it was a lack of respect for her efforts.

"Yes," said Mrs. Bill. "Tomorrow I believe I will discharge Mr. Pulver."

Jerry was frantic. He raised his voice. Gully would be crushed, he screamed. She was going straight to Hell, he assured her. Straight to sinner's Satan succulent Hell, where she would be rubbed between the Devil's fingers like a dirty match. Where she would hoe and hoe forever and not even a weed would sprout.

Mrs. Bill was shocked. Her son had never raised his voice to her like this since Mr. Bill had died. He had always known his place and known when to keep his mouth shut. His association with this Mr. Pulver had stifled his naturally submissive personality.

"You would do well," she warned, ignoring Jerry's flailing arms, "to keep silent on matters you know nothing about." If Jerry had not been an atheist, Mrs. Bill knew exactly what she would have done. "Jesus loves the humble of heart," she would have quoted from the Bible, "and you must honor thy mother as yourself." But there was no sense in discussing faith with the blind. Mrs. Bill was deeply hurt.

Jerry banged his way out of the parlor room and locked himself in his invention room, whimpering softly. He broodingly uncoiled the triple-K rope from its designated spot near the door, then yanked it between his hands and gnawed it with his teeth. He looked out the window down at the moonlit garden and saw Mrs. Bill tied to a huge, curved, iron plow by Gully with the very rope he was biting on. He covered her with honey and cockleburs. A headlight was strapped to her forehead. Gully butted Mrs. Bill from behind with his banana bike, and she trudged along like a machine, plowing her own damn garden, while Jerry bounced around the perimeters of the garden throwing handfuls of pennies at her face.

"Take that, you machine!" Jerry said.

Soon her cheeks were filled with deep silver scars. Broccoli florets writhed in her hair. Mushrooms bled from her false teeth.

"You killed my father, you filthy machine!" he said.

When his mother finally began crying and Gully's little legs were sore, Jerry went to his bedroom and threw himself into bed.

He fell asleep pretending to tell Gully about his father. Mr. Bill had died of anorexia nervosa nineteen years earlier, Jerry told Gully, long before any movie star had made it famous. When his father had gone off to the hospital to die for the last time, they invaded his body with more and more experimental tubes, until Jerry wasn't allowed to visit him anymore. As a child, Jerry dreamed of him again and again, always as a melting skeleton of a man in a wooden chair connected to a cold, gray machine by colorful, pulsating tubes and wires, his father's hooded eyelids bulging and winking shut like a frog's with each pulse of fluid through the tubes. Jerry woke from the dreams screaming. Mrs. Bill used to stand at the foot of his bed and listen to Jerry's screams in silence, then solemnly return to her own heavy slumber. Finally when Jerry was thirteen the dreams had stopped, and since then neither Jerry nor Mrs. Bill had mentioned them.

And now, the night before the last trick he could ever play on Gully, Jerry dreamed again of Mr. Bill. He and his father huddled on the rickety bleachers of a high school football stadium littered with vegetables, the sky glazed over with vanilla icing, dust blowing into their open mouths with each gust of wind. Jerry carried his father down the creaking bleachers, strapped him to the dolly, and wheeled him squeakily around the cinder track until they came to a large, humming radiator. They warmed themselves at the radiator, and Mr. Bill magically pulled long pussy willow branches and marshmallows from the pockets of his flannel shirt. Then Gully flew over them, high above the bleachers, skimming just below the tasty sky, flapping his fat arms and wheezing. They called to Gully to come down and roast marshmallows, but he kept circling around and around, ice falling from his chest in chunks. Mr. Bill looked up into Jerry's eyes and said, "Aren't we all each other's children?" Then his face became translucent and quietly melted into his skull, seeping entirely into his eye sockets with a quick, slurping sound. The radiator taxied across the football field, spraying lime over the sidelines, and flew after Gully, hissing a floating, obscure piano-tune from Jerry's childhood. Mrs. Bill sat in the pressbox above the bleachers like a dark, featureless stone.

"Come back," Jerry called out. "Come back!"

"Gerald, are you crying?" his mother said, standing at the foot of his bed.

Jerry blinked and sat up in bed, stunned fully awake.

"Mama!" he sobbed. "I had another dream about Dad!"

Mrs. Bill stood unmoving, with the moonlight streaming through the window just missing her face. Jerry's screams had awakened her from an unreflective sleep. She waited several seconds before speaking, calculating exactly what to say.

"Just close your eyes tight," she said, "and concentrate on the darkness."

It was the same advice she had given him when he was toilet training.

She shuffled back to her room in her bedroom slippers, and Jerry lay awake all night with her advice swishing back and forth in his head to the tune of an overly slow "Row, Row, Row, Your Boat."

Saturday morning Mrs. Bill jumped out of bed and greeted the sunny day with open arms. She bustled around her room putting on her work clothes, whistling to herself; she could almost feel her vegetables growing within her very soul. It was a perfect day for prayer, she thought. She envisioned herself standing under Jerry's window like Joan of Arc, wishing all of her enemies a blessed Saturday morning.

Jerry moved around his invention room mechanically, acting out of an impulse to make his final trick a lesson for

Gully that the boy would never forget. He had a firm sense of purpose now. Like a father. He had primed Gully for this day for weeks, adding fate, deputize, legitimist, tension, oppossum, languish, and sway to his list of "Words On His Mind." It was important that Gully realize their vital kinship now and understand the true stuff that magic was made of.

He nailed the edges of the naugahyde backing from his father's wheelchair to the bottom of the door as a brace, then strung the triple-K rope under the brace and double-knotted the rope around the inside doorknob of his invention room. He double checked to make sure the deadbolt was securely thrown, then pounded thirteen pennies all along the doorway between the door and the frame. Then he tapped all of the pins from the hinges. The door was now held in place only by the pennies and the deadbolt. He stood in the middle of the room and pulled on the rope, but both the brace and the door held. Then he wound the other end of the rope through the windows of the GOLDEN RULE radiator, and tied the rope back to itself in a triple friendship knot.

When Mrs. Bill left her praying beside the garden to answer Gully's knock at the parlor room door, Jerry lowered the extension ladder through the window, then climbed out onto it. He reached back into the room and heaved the radiator up to the windowsill, then carefully lowered it till it dangled out the window from the triple-K rope attached to his invention room door. The radiator hung from the creaking rope just a few feet below the windowsill, swaying back and forth like a reliable pendulum. One of the pennies popped from its place around the door frame, bowing to the tension. Jerry scrambled down the ladder and silently hung it back in the garage where it belonged. The ladder was not a regular fixture of his invention room.

When Jerry got to the parlor room, Gully looked strangely thin and deflated, as if Mrs. Bill had let all the air out of him with one jab of a pin. She handed him her final payment and told him she trusted that this would teach him a valuable lesson about responsibility. Then she bustled back to her gardening and prayer. Jerry put his hand on Gully's shaking shoulder, and Gully looked up into his eyes and beheld the strength there. Jerry was his father. A better father than he had ever had. Together they walked up the steps holding hands.

"This," whispered Jerry, "is my magic room. Inside you will find all that dreams are made of." He dangled the key to the invention room door in front of Gully's little face. On the door was the sign "Inventions . . . While You Wait" that Jerry had bought from Coco Bunner and hung for his mother's sake.

The key sang happily in Gully's hand as he inserted it into the keyhole. Jerry stepped back from the door and closed his eyes, picturing the scenario about to unfold. Gully would turn the key, throwing the dead bolt, and the weight of the GOLDEN RULE radiator would yank the invention room door across the room and send it crashing through the window. Then the suction would lift him and Gully through the window, and they would fly off together on top of the magic door to join his father and roast marshmallows forever.

When Gully turned the key in the lock Jerry's eyes yanked open. The door hung suspended for a moment, then fell forward with a small puff. Gully screamed in delight and clapped his hands over his mouth. Sunlight trumpeted through the open window across from the doorway, illuminating the frayed end of the broken triple-K rope lying on the dusty floor. It had not proven to be as reliable a rope as Coco had promised. The GOLDEN RULE radiator had dropped of its own weight.

Jerry glided over to the window, picked up the listless end of the broken rope, summoned a sufficient amount of remorse, and looked down over the windowsill at his mother. She lay thickly next to the garden, steam rising from her body. The radiator had struck her squarely on the forehead; her end had been instant and unthinking. Gully slipped up under Jerry's arm as Jerry stared down at his mother, his eyes brimming over in a paroxysm of ice, trickling down to melt all of his radiator dreams asleep.

FIGURATIVE LANGUAGE: BRIDGING THE SCIENTIFIC-RHETORICAL-RAT GAP

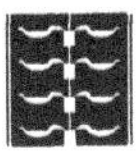

The University of New Jersey
1415 Science Road
Vorhees, New Jersey 08062

School of Arts and Sciences — **Area Code 609**
Department of Psychology — **267-4000**

April 1, 1990

Verna Hoffer
Department of English
The Pennsylvania State University
University Park, PA 16802

Dear Ms. Hoffer:
Thank you for your interesting and unusual letter of a few months ago. Although it was a passionate and generic form letter, I'm taking the time to make a controlled personal response. My colleagues are right now sitting in the coffee room and scoffing at me for doing this—they have shredded their copies of your letter and given them to the rats.

I must challenge you on the point that the scientific community of which I am a member writes in an "unprofessional, slip-shod way which breeds inhumanity." Although I am now studying to be a behavioral therapist, I hold a degree in English myself, and I assure you that I can turn a nifty phrase and trump up a sentence with just as much laconic style as you. The difference between us is that I understand my work and you do not. I, and my colleagues, use the rat as a test subject, not because we are bound by, as you call it, a "tradition of absurdity" (a phrase, by the way, which applies itself more readily to *your* field than to mine), but because we are *devoted to knowledge*, and rats' brains have the same constituents, the same chemicals, and the same basic neural connections as our own brains do.[1] Rats' brains are differentiated from ours only by cortex size and overall shape, and thus they are excellent models for study. As early as 350 B.C., Aristotle (a guy I'll bet you've fawned over now and again) dissected live animals in the pursuit of scientific study. But I don't expect you to understand this. Although it is true, as you mentioned, that some experimenters at our Head Injury Clinic were being protested against for awhile, their research *simulated* the effects of auto accidents on cats via artificial means—they didn't actually drive the cats around mercilessly in a car and crash them into a brick wall (as the analogy in your form letter would lead one to think), but *controlled* the brain damage to the cats in the *laboratory* in order to examine neurological results of injury and develop more effective treatment strategies for human car accident victims. Naturally, my colleagues and I harden our hearts against your kind of uninformed, self-serving criticism.

[1]Thus science uncovers parallels: quail, poisoned by blue, sour water, afterwards avoid *blue* but not sour; rats, poisoned by blue sour water, afterwards, like man, avoid *sour* but not blue.

I must *thank* you, however, for prodding me into writing a paper that has been gnawing at me for some time. As a first-year graduate student, I've been struggling to nestle into my own niche in the scientific-academic community, and I think you've helped me find a way to "bed down." Your letter prompted me to write up the attached study (my first graduate paper), in which I put into practice your suggestion that we "courageously tell the world the truth about [our] work, instead of hiding behind obscure, degrading, speciesist language." I am sending the attached study out to the *Journal of Experimental Psychology* for possible publication. It is impeccably researched and I am enthusiastic about it; I hope that it also helps to correct some of your misguided notions about animal experimentation, especially in regards to the rat. Again, thank you.

Albert Frick

Figurative Language:
Bridging the Scientific-Rhetorical-Rat Gap

Albert Frick
The University of New Jersey

ABSTRACT

This paper examines the partial results of a behavioral study of Norway rats—specifically concerning one rat which behaved in a rather unruly yet fascinating fashion. The original intention of this research was to test the theory that rats, when exposed over time to inescapable shock, will accomplish complete passivity even when forcibly prompted to rise. Many studies have proven that rats are capable of both *learned helplessness* and surprising eccentric behavior,[2] and this study resembles those in that it is designed to provoke a lever-pulling response from the rats' amazingly durable little paws. The real contribution of the current writing, however, comes in its presentation of a new *communication theory*, especially useful to those researchers who are faced with both criticism from outside parties and the problem of reluctant and often vexing test subjects, both rats and

---

[2]Two recent examples from the same journal will suffice:

Devenport and Holloway, "The Rat's Resistance to Superstition: Role of the Hippocampus." *Journal of Comparative and Physiological Psychology*. 1980. Vol. 94, No. 4. 691-705. ***This study illustrated that rats, unlike pigeons, seem immune to the development of superstition in their lever-pulling habits.***

Dohanich and Ward. "Sexual Behavior in Male Rats Following Intra-cerebral Estrogen Application." *Journal of Comparative and Physiological Psychology*. 1980. Vol. 94, No. 4. 712-722. ***This study found that estrogen injections induce males to superstitiously attempt mating behavior even after castration.***

otherwise. The resulting rhetorical principles that have been evolved will be peppered throughout the syntax of this study, and are even evidenced subtly in this abstract.

I. INTRODUCTION

In recent years, a lot of attention has been focused on the issue of the "morality" of animal experimentation. Most recently, the House of Representatives has heard an amendment to section 19 of the Animal Welfare Act which will allow "private" citizens (if there are such beings) to sue organizations which they feel are violating the act.[3] Thus, attacks by "animal rights" groups flood our mailboxes, and we are even accused of promoting an "immoral vocabulary" about animals which reveals our allegedly black and adrenal hearts, while thumping our own Darwinian chests ape-like in defense of scientific advancement.[4] The underlying problem is twofold: as behavioral scientists we must objectively record only observable and noteworthy behavior; as human beings we admire aesthetics. The outcome: a seeming robotic diction which is admirable for its clinical purity, but marks a low notch on the creative yardstick. This writer—who holds a B.A. in English and is now pursuing and M.S. in Psychology—has spent the last few months doing a behavioral study on rats, and thus is particularly sensitive to the need for appeasing both the behavioral scientist and the whining "animal rights" aesthete

---

[3]See Report by the Committee on the Judiciary, House of Representatives. H.R. 1770. September 16, 1988. Serial No. 76.

[4]Some diction taken from a form letter written by one Ms. Verna Hoffer, the Pennsylvania State University.

by writing in the cleanest and the most pleasing language possible.

At a cocktail party, a respected American writer once said, "For me, the Holocaust and a corncob are the same."[5] This clever little equation makes it clear that language, by definition, allows equity among all subject matter. Further, language itself is divorced from morality: whether evoking a mound of seared flesh or a docile dinner plate, the written word reflects the subjectivity of the *reader* more than that of the writer. Yet we scientists meticulously cloak ourselves in the language of the lab coat while our readers, both professional and otherwise, know perfectly well that we are waking, walking, moral beings, with cozy fireplaces and curled-up kittens at home. The scientist-as-citizen may torture his ferret without purpose and properly be called immoral, but the scientist-as-writer is recording observable and historical facts, and thus morality is not the real issue.

We should, therefore, strive to make our writing both clinically accurate and prudently artistic, especially considering the *subjective nature* of the "animal rights" persons who peruse our journals in search of rhetorical atrocities. The suggestion provided herein is to use *figurative language*—to cast our experimental animals in subjective, flattering, and artistic language where appropriate, but without violating scientific purity. Thus a rat's stripped belly can properly be said to be "portly" rather than "substantial," then later be called "smelly" instead of "effluvial." The net effect will be a creative pacifying of *both* our audiences: to the reader demanding "equality" for the rats, we offer, through language, quiet applause for the rats'

[5]See Ozick, Cynthia. "Innovation and Redemption: What Literature Means." *Art and Ardor*. New York: Alfred A. Knopf, 1983. 238-248.

considerable contributions to science;[6] to our fellow scientists, we report with innovation and publicly juice their pens to respond in kind. Such technique is, after all, more fluent, and has even crept naturally into the writing of such respected scientists as Martin Seligman; Seligman tells how, after fifty trials, the best dogs will leap across a barrier *gracefully* in order to avoid moderate-to-severe shock.[7] On principle, if it's good enough for Seligman it should be good enough for everyone. Some might argue that the use of *figurative language* will curb the level of objectivity necessary to our work, but this writer urges such skeptics to honestly assess the rhetorical achievement which this paper embodies, then see if you, too, don't wish to write in this new, neat way.

A further modification in our writing is also suggested: let's cut back on the passive voice and courageously assert our identity within our work. The damnably overrated use of the passive voice dates back to the 1920's[8] and we witness the unflappable practice of the experimenter avoiding the personal pronoun "I" in everything from technical journals to modern fiction.[9] It has become painfully obvious that the passive voice is often a rowboat concealed inside of an ark—an itty-bitty individual denying his wee selfhood in favor of joint membership in the already overpopulated human species. The

---

[6]In addition to their use in the Behavioral Sciences, rats have been used generously to help combat aging, cancer, and diabetes, to name just a few. For an extended report of the rat's prolific contributions to biomedical research, see *Health Benefits of Animal Research,* edited by William I. Gay, D.V.M. Published by the Foundation for Biomedical Research. 1985.

[7]See Seligman, Martin E.P. *Helplessness: On Depression, Development, and Death.* University of Pennsylvania: Wilt Freeman and Company. 1975. 22.

[8]See Tichy, H.J. "Advice to Scientist-Writers: Beware Old Fallacies." *The Scientist.* October 31, 1988. 17.

[9]See, for example, Hemingway, Ernest, *The Nick Adams Stories.* New York: Charles Scribner's Sons. 1972.

passive voice *does* function admirably when we are presenting our experimental methods, but the sad truth is that by avoiding the word "I" we are subduing authorial pride when we should be awarding ourselves credit, and our unfriendly "animal-loving" readers perch like hoot owls and screech "Who? Who? Who? Who wrote this?" into the yawning abyss of our authorial canyons. In short, passive voice and depersonalized pronouns have both become cliché, and the use of "I" allows the researcher to boldly assert his identity within an esoteric environment where it is becoming increasingly difficult both to affirm one's own importance and innovatively test the rat.[10] I also find it invigorating to smarten up experimental reporting with tropes and schemes—in particular, metaphor, anthimeria, paradox, and litote. Let us be equally conscious of using plain language in favor of technospeak at times: we're all familiar with the too-popular phrase—"the biota exhibited a 100% mortality response"—when it is equally accurate and infinitely more satisfying to write "all the fish died."[11] In short: let us

---

[10]This approach allows me to compete, philosophically speaking, with some of the more sophisticated recent studies. For example:

Taylor, Griffin, and Rupich. "Conspecific Urine Marking in Male Rats (Rattus norvegicus) Selected for Relative Aggressiveness." *Journal of Comparative Psychology*. 1988. Vol. 102. 72-77. *The research discovered that aggressive rats—whether injected with fluorescein solution or not—deposited urine on conspecifics more prolifically than nonaggressive rats made similar deposits.*

Pilz, Schnitzler, and Menne. "Acoustic Startle Threshold of the Albino Rat." *Journal of Comparative Psychology*. 1987. Vol. 101. 67-72. *The research revealed that freeroaming naive rats in a ballistic chamber had higher levels of startle-response to acoustic signals than did hammock-restrained naive rats in the same setting.*

Standards in Laboratory Animal Management. England: Universities Federation Animal Welfare. 1984. 14. *The research shows that temperatures of 34-43° C can cause death and sterility, impaired lactation, and depression of foetal and neonatal growth in rats.*

[11]From Thompson, Edward T. "How to Write Clearly." Published by International Paper Company, New York.

be bold wordsmiths, wheeling our way into *all* of our readers' minds and myths.

The original intention of my experiment was simple: to determine if rats, after reaching a state of *learned helplessness*, could be returned to their original naive (untrained) state, and again actively seek to avoid shock. Seligman successfully achieved this restoration of naive behavior in dogs,[12] and when my research is completed, I eventually intend to attempt the same kind of restoration in the surviving rats. But as you've guessed by now, my essential contribution to the current research really comes via language, and the actual "rat end" of the experiment is still in progress. This particular paper was inspired by an unusually shrewd and elusive rat, whom I shall give a proper name later in the text. This rat, though only one among the seventeen who unfortunately have thus far died during my experiment, exhibited such an uncommon response to behavioral therapy that I will not touch upon it until later in this paper, where there will be sufficient space for expansion.

II. METHODS

Shuttleboxes

The thirty-eight shuttleboxes for the rats were painted with Cresodip to repel lice. Each box was made from a standard dormer cage and measured 3 feet x 2 feet to provide the rats with

---

[12]See Seligman, Martin E.P. *Helplessness: On Depression, Development, and Death.* University of Pennsylvania: Wilt Freeman and Company. 1975. *When 100 of Seligman's dogs had achieved learned helplessness in the shuttleboxes and thus refused to jump the barriers to escape shock, Seligman removed the barriers from the boxes and forcibly dragged the dogs to the safe sides of the shuttleboxes 25 to 200 times—until about two-thirds of them were actually able to relearn the original behavior of gracefully leaping the shuttlebox barriers to escape shock.*

ample room for stretching and running in little circles.[13] A six-inch high metal partition was secured in the center of each shuttlebox which the rat could vault if desired.

Electric Current

In the shuttlebox grid floors, an electric current of 40 volts was supplied for sixty-second intervals every thirteen or ninety minutes, depending on the time of day. The metal partition was electrified as well because Hunter found that a rat will actually perch competently on the shuttlebox partition to try to escape shock.[14] The front screens of each cage were also charged continuously with 20 volts to discourage the mutinous behavior of screen-clinging.

Reinforcement Levers

Two reinforcement levers were provided in the back of each shuttlebox—one red lever and one green lever; one on either side of the partition. On the even-numbered days of the experiment, the green levers had to be depressed 100 times between each shock for the rats to receive positive reinforcement, while the red levers had to be depressed only 50 times. On the odd-numbered days of the experiment, the conditions were reversed.[15]

---

[13]Note that I consulted a veterinarian in determining an adequate shuttlebox size, as required by the Animal Welfare Act—*even though it does not apply to rats.*
[14]Hunter, W.S. "Conditioning and Extinction in the Rat." *British Journal of Psychology.* 1935. Volume 26. 135-148.
[15]The reasoning here should be obvious: If the task were not rather difficult, the rat, unlike members of other species, would perform it successfully each time. I was testing the theory that rats would learn that one lever was preferable to another on certain days, but then would discover *learned helplessness* and finally choose to make no distinction between the levers at all, finally lying passively during the shocks regardless of which side of the shuttlebox housed them. This particular experimental design was developed because, historically, the rat has

Feeding and Watering

Positive reinforcement was provided through separate water and feed ducts, which opened and emptied one ounce of water and one ounce of Purina Lab Chow into each shuttlebox at the same time that the electrical shocks were administered. If and when the rats didn't have the gumption to depress the levers the required number of times, the electrical shock was provided without the feeding and watering.

Figurative Language

I cannot take complete credit for realizing the power of *figurative language.* I was inspired, in part, by the writing of Alain Robbe-Grillet. He helped me to see that, like metaphor, *figurative language* is never an "innocent figure of speech."[16] When we say that a rat's behavior is "capricious" or that he "huddles" in his cage, we are not, and we can not, simply be recording physical data—we are choosing analogical vocabulary that reveals, as Robbe-Grillet calls it, "an entire metaphysical system"—and it's this system which our scientific-creative minds have been charged with stewardship of. *Figurative language* does not make us one with the rats or make them one with us; rather, it whirls us further into the embrace of science, while keeping the rats at arm's length by forcing us to really *look* at them, refurbish them in the purest terms we can muster, listen to their lessons, and *witness their existence.*

---

proven to be a much craftier test-subject than the dog in terms of *learned helplessness,* and the new designs are highly valued.

[16]For a more lengthy discussion of the true nature of metaphor, refer to Robbe-Grillet, Alain. *For a New Novel.* Evanston, Illinois: Grove Press Inc. 1965. 53-55.

While watching over the laudable behavior of the favored rat in my experiment, *figurative language* became especially appropriate. I developed a Figurative Words Log of over 200 entries so far, *just using adjectives and nouns,* that we can begin assigning to the rat, and I'm starting to get a handle on the verbs and adverbs as well. Here is an excerpt from my log which lends itself nicely to the rat:

Typical Scientific Adjective	*Figurative Alternative*
trifling	heroic
hooded	decorous
naive	pristine
helpless	autonomous
phlegmatic	seasoned
emotional	errant

Typical Scientific Noun	*Figurative Alternative*
trauma	incompletion
sacrifice	servitude
lesion	sacrifice
safe	tranquil
stress	spiritedness
death	grace

Of course, care must be taken so that the figurative words chosen are used with consistency and discretion, and different experimenters will have different preferences.

III. RESULTS

After voiding the rats' bladders via soft paint brushes inserted into their anogenital areas to rid them of impurities and ensure relative equality among them, I began the experiment by placing the rats in the shuttleboxes—one per box. After just two weeks, most rats displayed the classic symptoms of the early stages of *learned helplessness*: prolific amounts of excretion (defecation *and* urination), spirited head-shaking, dainty paw-padding, superstitious leaping, open sleeplessness, durable "box-lapping," upside down doggie paddling, posing or freezing when touched, seasoned huddling in a cage corner, and errant, indiscriminate lever-pressing.

One rat, though, which I shall now name "Max" ("Greatest in Excellence")[17] did something unprecedented. For four days, Max[18] clung adamantly to the front of his cage, even though the screen he clutched was under constant electrical charge, and he squinted at me mysteriously like an animal—or pseudo-animal—from one of Poe's fictions.[19] Max seemed at once servile and tranquil: arching his back in the manner of either sexual tease or feigned agony. He bobbed his head continually yet also exuded some sort of contrived motor-pattern that I couldn't quite put my finger on.[20] He screeched an odd "aeaaka, aeaaka" sound and occasionally pounded his nose

---

[17]From Rule, Lareina. *Name Your Baby*. New York: Bantam Books. 1966. 164.

[18]By the way, this name was not chosen, as some readers may be tempted to think, to resemble the "Max" in John Barth's *Giles Goat-Boy* (1966). Any resemblance is purely coincidental.

[19]I am reminded of "The Black Cat," "Hop-Frog: or, the Eight Charmed Ourang-Outangs," Pym's faithful dog "Tiger," and, of course, "The Raven."

[20]I first suspected that Max might be an offspring of the strain of rats developed by Ward's experiments on chronic stress (*Psychopathology: Experimental Models*. ed. Martin E.P. Seligman. University of Pennsylvania: W.H. Freeman and Company. 1977. 397-399.) in which pregnant female rats were placed into tight Plexiglas containers illuminated by floodlights. The male pups of these mothers ended up acting very strangely indeed, but Max could not have been an heir of these. In fact, I found out that Max was brought in by one of my colleagues, who had removed him from his neighbor's basement.

against the screen with all his might. He was, in fact, so obviously lively and tyrannical that his very manner said "*I will not learn.*" While most of his caged peers were busy being either docile or hyperaggressive within just a few yards of him, Max alone clung to the electrically charged screen in a state of utter incompletion.

I decided to meet his challenge. By day, I held "stare-downs" with him to try to hold his attention and freeze him in place, but he remained always in motion—a flexion here, a quiver there. Even when he seemed to stop I could see that his fur was bristling, and he bared his teeth and hissed right at me just when I thought he was tuckered out. He made me feel at odds with myself. In the evenings I pondered, read a lot, and found comfort in the histories of others who had been openly challenged with similar forms of aggressive skepticism.[21] Still, I found myself perplexed.

On Day Three of Max's clinging, even stranger things began to happen. As though he knew I was keeping tabs on him with *figurative language* in my mind, Max did odd things to purposely pique my mind-pen: he hung upside-down and gnawed his long incisors viciously on the screen bottom; he

---

[21]To quote from *Helplessness* (Seligman, 1975, 170): "Richter reasoned that being held in the hand of a predator like man, having whiskers trimmed, and being put in a vat of water from which escape is impossible produces a sense of helplessness in the rat. This must have sounded like a radical speculation to his tough-minded readers, but he substantiated it."

Also, just one month after William Faulkner was blackballed from the Scribblers of Sigma Upsilon—an Oxford campus literary society—because of his "airs," a series of parodies of his early poetry began to appear in the Oxford campus newspaper, the first of which transmogrified Faulkner's seductive maiden of "Naiads' Song" into a barnyard animal. (See Michael Grimwood's *Heart in Conflict: Faulkner's Struggle with Vocation.* 1987. 25.)

On a more personal note: one of my mother's favorite sayings was "those who coolly eye the tiger need not fear the fang."

coolly wiggled his ears for hours; he scraped his belly from side to side until it was raw and filled with sacrifice scars; he thrust his tail straight out through a screen-hole, blatantly wagging it in long, seductive whips. In short, Max acted completely pristine and sexual, stirring in me the bizarre notion that he was both my slave and my intimate—I his lord-brother, his hangman-lover. That night I dreamed of Max heaping himself upon me, chilling my heart, writhing on my throat, his cold lips seeking mine, and then falling back into a lounge chair and holding his belly thick with laughter, assuring me that it was all a simple jest between two friends.[22] When I woke I realized that Max stirred something unnerving and neighborly in me—mocked by his unctuous gaze, I felt overwhelmed with the simple fact of *being alive.*[23] Momentarily, I had the

---

[22]See Poe's "The Pit and the Pendulum."

[23]Strangely, this sort of thing has happened to me before. In seventh grade, Mrs. Dilker showed us an experiment that proved frogs are sometimes not smart enough to jump out of water. First, she stuck a frog in a pan of boiling water and it leapt right out, slipping out of her hands and off the high black tabletop onto the floor, and causing a merry flurry through the room as girls shrieked into their pigtails, boys flung their sharpened pencils and metal rulers to the floor, hoping to draw blood and see if it was really green; Mrs. Dilker high-stepped among the scraping chairs, batting at her feet with a broom, and spiral notebooks fluttered over our heads, snowing little bits of soft,. curled notebook paper into our hair. Then, when she caught the frog, Mrs. Dilker showed us how it padded around happily for a while in a pan of water at room temperature, and didn't even try to jump out as the water was heated to boiling—it just sat there, oblivious of its churning blood, bulging its eyes out and pumping its long throat back and forth more and more rapidly, the water around it rolling into bubbles that were clear, then white, then green, then pink.

One more incident occurs to me too. One sunny afternoon, when I was sixteen and driving alone for the first time, I saw a rabbit dart out from the bushes and dive right under my spinning left tire, prompting that familiar thump of bone-crushed-below which sickened my heart in those days. I stopped and watched the rabbit in the rearview mirror. It flickered up four-feet high off the ground, its body twisted and its head mashed red, with some neural

irrational thought of taking Max home and making a pet of him,[24] sitting with him at the kitchen table over a breakfast of eggs, bacon, toast, and orange juice.[25]

Keep in mind that this was not ordinary behavior for me. I wear sensible shoes, plant them firmly on the ground, and drive a Saab, yet watching over Max made my mind reel a bit and sparked both my creative and scientific instincts simultaneously. For three days, I watched and recorded subjective data in fascination while Max continued his antics, showing visible signs of paradoxical behavior: emitting wild squeals while seeming to hold his very breath; bleeding from the anus and bending around acrobatically to nonchalantly lick the blood from the tail; showing no normal wholesale reaction to the continuous electrical charge coursing through his body, yet looking, as much as a rat can, forlorn, servile, graceful, and sincere. These particular observations, I argue, are a direct

---

connection obviously awry, but the brain still somehow alive, telling the body to keep spinning, spinning, spinning, and not give in, then it landed and kicked off the macadam again, spitting something off to the side this time, and flopped up and down a few more times like an elastic fish, until I whirred the car backwards and crunched it under the same tire.

These are two of my sharpest memories, and they illustrate, I think, how moved we can be by animals at times, and how profoundly their haphazard fates remind us of our own fragile and privileged existence.

[24]Odd, but not unheard of. See West, Paul. *Rat Man of Paris*. New York: Macmillan Publishing Company. 1986. *Poulsifer, the Rat Man, houses a rat in a doll-house, then removes it and conceals it in his coat, profiteering by giving tourists an occasional peek as he strolls around Paris.*

Less fictionally, see Hendrickson, Robert. *More Cunning Than Man*. New York: Stein and Day Publishers. 1983. *The famous petite but well-kept Rat Woman of Miami lived with over 500 rats in her bungalow, feeding them lettuce and corn, until police ordered all the rats killed and the Rat Woman told them that people bothered her a lot more than rats ever did.*

[25]Interestingly, rats manufacture large doses of vitamin C in their bodies all by themselves and thus have no external need for it. See Paton, William. *Man and Mouse*. New York: Oxford University Press. 1984. 125.

result of my unique approach to this study: without the use of "I," I could not have recorded many of these significant experimental results; without Max's incredible behavior, there would be no reason to single him out; without *figurative language*, there would be no Max.

On Day Four, Max refused to move at all and simply clinched at a 45° angle to the screen, his claws frozen in place, his eyes vaguely fixed on a point somewhere in front of him, his tail curled in a frozen half-switch. I stared back as into a mirror—at once mystified, enraptured, appalled, and uplifted.

On Day Five, I opened Max's cage and pried his stiff form off the screen. He fell from my hand onto his back on the cage's latticed grid-floor, looking for all the world like he was waiting to be barbequed over the shredded paper and his own ammonia-filled droppings, rolling rigidly from side to side, like one of those Weeble-toys that happily rocks back and forth but refuses ever to fall down.

IV. DISCUSSION

Fondly, I am reminded once again of Martin Seligman's master work on helplessness. In one of my favorite chapters, Seligman captures the beautiful scientific paradox that continually embraces our work. First he tells, in a *seemingly* clinical and dispassionate way, how his own three-month-old son is suckling at his wife's breast in typical behavior/response patterns even as his father writes his book.[26] Just a few pages later, Seligman *lyrically* presents the ongoing enigmatic paradigm of *uterine* and *rearing* factors in rats: When pregnant

[26]Seligman, Martin E.P. *Helplessness: On Depression, Development, and Death.* University of Pennsylvania: Wilt Freeman and Company. 1975. 139.

rats who have been offered inescapable shock eventually give birth, do their pups show unnatural fears because the fears were transferred through the magic of the *womb*, or are the fears *learned* through the mother's obviously incompetent rearing habits? The studies designed to settle this issue, and the melding of the scientific with the aesthetic, continue.

Finally, I hope I have clarified the point that the compelling subtleties of *figurative language* implicit in Seligman's work and explicit in my own work are frank, inspiring, humane, and, in the end, sublime.

And so I leave you with the tortured and lofty image of Max: hovering belly-flat against his cage in the shape of a cross—blunt nose lifted to the heavens, hairy ears flattened back in supplication, outstretched paws fanned and forgiving, chest swelling triumphant above mangy stomach, feet dangling underneath in utter helplessness, and tail cocked at its elbow, seemingly ready to strike at those who dare look closer.

MEDIACRITY

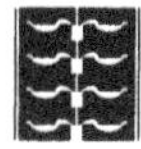

I know you thought you'd heard all there was to know about my wife by now, but I'm here to give you the inside scoop. My wife was a typical New York divorced woman well before we were divorced. She jumped from career to career like a frog on a mating spree. First she ran the famous Alfred E. Packer Student Union Grill at New York University, named after the only man ever convicted of cannibalism in the United States. Those were the good days. She even let me quote her in my first interview, which I published in a local leaflet. "Our grill," she said, "has consistently striven to attain the high standards exemplified by the life of Mr. Packer. Plus we're cheap."

Then things went sour. The FDA shut down the grill and she became a topless cellist, then produced a Marcel Marceau album, then gave brandy rubdowns and set that old man on fire—which you probably heard about—and generally she got into that whole New York spontaneous cult Darryl Hannah Legal Eagles *Doonesbury* esoteric environmental art thing. You know. Every week she had a new display of atrocities for her upcoming environmental art party. A one-act play in our living room called for me to club her with Buford Pussor's bat. I did it, but with chagrin. Finally, it got to the point where I just couldn't take it anymore. The last straw was Hitler's actual toilet seat, purchased at an auction, that she did a Hiroshima thing with. She hung the seat from a wooden fishing pole stuck into the toilet bowl, and somehow caused an explosion in the toilet with cleaning fluid, which set the pole on fire, then she dropped a big, breakable balloon full of baby powder in the middle of the bathroom floor, and as the dust settled everybody clapped and cried.

When she was finally arrested by the Fire Marshal, I moved out of the apartment and tried to publish a human interest piece about her as a cult figure, but the campus newspaper turned it down. "That woman," the Fire Marshal said to me, "has one leg in this world and one leg on the moon, and between these two legs she's got nothing to stand on."

So she got religion. And I got famous. As you might recall, she gave birth to our son Joshua a few months later. She went on Geraldo, and that was the first time she publicly insisted that I wasn't responsible for Joshua's birth.

"No, no, there was no conception," she told everyone. "It was divine intervention. Joshua is the new Messiah, and my husband is simply the vessel through which Joshua will attend school."

"We hear that your husband is quite a writer," Geraldo said.

"He is nothing like Joshua," she said. "Joshua came from the atmosphere, from the thing the astronauts see from the space shuttle and have to fight against when they leave the earth."

Oprah started dropping by my new place with questions, slipped me some money so she'd have an inside track on my wife, and my writing became famous. Mr. Downey called. I smiled a lot.

Then my wife put in a bid on the PTL Club and the real scandal began. Carlos Pepe Garcia, a Spanish religious fanatic who claimed that he could walk on water, also wanted to buy the PTL. Carlos called a special press conference to debate whether or not Joshua was the true new Messiah, hoping to publicly denounce my wife and Joshua at the same time. By this time, I was, of course, her ex-husband, and one among a cluster of reporters scribbling notes with fascination.

"Let them behold the truth," Carlos said loudly to my wife, sweeping his arm at my sea of colleagues and me. "Tell them of the son Joshua wetting the sheets. He lies in bed with distress. Tell them it."

"Joshua is God's child," she countered calmly. "His urine represents mortality. It comes from the stars. Your jealousy leers its ugly head because you're often immersed in wetness yourself but not as famous as Joshua."

"Quiet the woman," said Carlos, flailing his arms for the cameras, "she befouls my name."

"Every year," my wife explained to us, "Carlos Pepe Garcia sinks in the ocean with a surprised look on his face."

"The son is a bedwetter and he stutters the words," Carlos cursed.

"Every year," my wife insisted, drinking in our attention, "Carlos says he will walk on water and he is fished from the sea like a dead sheep. He pays reporters to come and write about the miracle of his fat body sinking under the surface. Five years in a row now."

"It is the fault of the press!" Carlos said, causing a stir among us. "They refuse to record the history in proper form and I lose concentration. It is the flashbulbs! They are like weights to my feet."

"They won't shut up about my son Joshua either," my wife said, smiling slyly for the camera.

"For me, next year will be noted," said Carlos, snatching back the spotlight. "I will hover over the ocean waters. I meditate and diet each day. Men will be awed."

"I believe you will make it!" I shouted, drawing a protest from the other reporters.

"Shut up," said Carlos. "The reporter cares nothing of religion. To you religion is a puppet to use as ridicule for the believers. You know nothing of the symbol. To you a fish is for eating only. You write of the fisherman who is choked by the jumping fish off the hook, but you miss its symbolic story."

"Listen well to him," my wife said. "He is our authority on fish, since he spends so much time with them. A whale has adopted him."

"Silence the woman," said Carlos, pointing dramatically. "She makes filthy the symbol. She seeks only the printed words."

The remainder of the conference is a blur to me. I stopped taking notes and basked in the wealth of my wife's wonder. She was pure and contemporary and newsworthy, embodying all that I ever dreamed of writing about. I was in love.

THAT THIN LINE

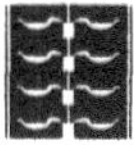

Some said I was a witch. I let them believe as they wished. To tease them, I knelt at the picture window each weekday at 3:08 p.m. when the schoolchildren came, flailing my arms and chomping my teeth, gnashing wild and artistic with none of them realizing that I was really flashing a grin. They saw me: a hideous, interesting mouth surrounded by a wreath of streaked, brittle hair pulled back from the face with a blue rubber band and a few bobby pins, rubbing my head against the wool curtains so that my hair loosened and stood on end snakelike and mysterious. Often, a girl's face was jammed flat and distorted against the glass opposite me by her schoolmates. She was all nostril and eyebrow and lip, squirming and squeaking red against my window, only three centimeters away, begging for entry. Her schoolmates beat on the glass and hooted at me—this woman they admired because she drilled holes and laid hexes and dissected lunch boxes with her eyes.

I say she's a witch, they said.

Can she talk? they wondered.

Is she sick? they screamed.

Then the mothers and fathers dragged them off and I closed the curtains and guffawed at their youth.

Inside the curtains, I was not a witch, but a walking climacteric. Climacteric was a much better term for my condition than menopause. Menopause was for the masses, interruptive and universal; climacteric was much more like a true climax: four, quick, permanent thuds to my body, squeezing it into something more boxlike. I could say, "I am my climacteric," but I couldn't say "I am my menopause"—it sounded ridiculous. I walked, breathed, reeked climacteric; I wallowed in climacteria; I thought climacteranically.

Years ago, as soon as I had accustomed myself to having gobs of ova rolling down my thighs each month, finally convinced my body was only replenishing itself ritualistically instead of falling away in meaty clumps, I was informed: You're just going through menopause. The doctor told me I would perspire less and nap more often. He told me my periods would no longer matter. He did not tell me I would miss them.

So I developed my own system. Every forty days, I starved myself for seventy-two hours, drinking only fatty milk, until all I could think about was that thin line of hunger coiling sideways through my head and esophagus, and I smelled myself claylike and metallic and thick: the smells of my menstruation. If I starved myself again before forty days passed, I collapsed, so my limited tolerance and some controlled experimentation created a natural forty-day cycle between each of my three-day menstrual periods. This system put me well ahead of the planets, making all my months exactly forty-three days long and my years five-hundred-sixteen days long (43 x 12 = 516). In theory, I found this system much more satisfactory than the old one. I calculated one of the advanges on a chart.

CHART

MY CYCLE		LUNAR CYCLE	
516		365	
x 4		x 4	
=2064	days	=1460	days
+ 0	Leap Days	+ 1	Leap Day
=2064	days	=1461	days

2064
- 1461
=603 days

This put me six-hundred-three days ahead of everyone else every four years. My plan was to get so far ahead of everyone else that I would become younger rather than older. The schoolchildren knew nothing of this, but I foolishly told Max.

Max was a man. Like all men, he displayed his true weakness only at thc urinal in the public restroom where he cried and picked his nose when no one was watching. My job was to bang on the door and tell Max to hurry up and take a piss. He was my little lizard, waiting for me to pat his scaly head and tell him he'd been a good pet. He was a burglar, breaking the padlock on my cellar doors each night and strolling into my living room, posing as a welcome guest. He was as bubbly and boring as a cup of Alka-Seltzer.

According to Max, he was none of these things, but simply an expert on the ways of cats. To illustrate, he lay on his back in the middle of my living room, paddling all four limbs in the air and shimmying his spine, explaining that this was the cat's most secure fighting position. He noted that Figure 1, "The Skeleton of the Cat," was mislabeled: number 30, the so-called *medial malleolus*, was actually the *metacarpus*. A common pedestrian error, he told me. He explained how practical a cat's shoulderblades were, and practiced his Panther-step, arching his belly as he crawled down the basement steps. He spent his days wandering the streets looking for stray cats to add to his collection in my basement, or studying catbooks and encyclopedias in the library, or switching the feminine hygiene and fruit juices and toothpaste signs in the aisles of supermarkets. Max was an idiot.

Max had one mission: to lure me into the sack with his intellect. To that end, he deposited 3" x 5" index cards around my house in assorted locations, occasionally shoving them rudely into my hands and interrupting me while I was

GET READY FOR THE MAX-CAT DICTIONARY© (FIRST EDITION) FOR YOU (partial)

This note from Max introduced a flurry of index cards which, supposedly, were part of a special dictionary of catwords he was compiling for publication. Really, they were the slices he scratched into my back, interrupting the harmony of what used to be a perfectly vibrant torso.

catacombs (kăt´uh-kōmz´) *pl.n.* A structure of hexagonal, thin-walled, private cells formulated from loose cat hair by Max in the basement.

This index card was stuck to the top of an empty honeyjar in my kitchen. I scoffed secretly, but told Max that it was quite tasty. I humored him regularly, pretending to listen to his jabbering about the "surreal" as he squatted in the basement doorway and observed the cats while they mated. Max was generally so fascinated by their mating that he felt compelled to put his hand over my left breast. As usual, I looked at him rigidly and he called me a witch.

If I was a witch, as Max insisted, then the cats he stored in my basement were the Devil's emissaries, and they came to me at night to scratch the blood which bound me to Satan, sucking from my extra teats for comfort, as Max would never be allowed to do. At midnight I held mysterious conclaves and danced wildly with cats tied to my petticoats by their tails. I was Mother Tabbyskins, teaching my kittens how to spit and scold and gobbling up the doctor because I was violently ill and hungry. Of course, I told Max none of this. I told him to get his damn paw off my tit.

To distract myself from Max's insistent hands, I concentrated on the little blue oval I imagined on my breastplate, four fingers down from my larynx, where my cleavage used to begin. This was the center of my universe. From my oval, thin antennae crept out over my ribs, and no one could see them but me. My oval was an exotic brooch with wavy feelers which sprang up out of the earth and through my chest, protecting me from the hands of men, or a spider with tentacles which fondled me affectionately and slurped my juices through my skin.

Most women enjoy being touched by men there, Max complained as I removed his hand.

Within my oval was a small circle of soft teeth, suctioning my finger gently down into my trachea and through a funnel and into the left ventricle of my heart, where I touched a tiny, pulsing doorknob which no one else knew about—a fibrous button smeared with a film of fluid, pouring elixir-like through the soft copper tubing of my arteries and returning back to my finger to spawn. Deep inside my oval I became egglike and reeked of cytoplasm. I was fertile again.

Of course, Max understood none of this. I explained carefully to him that we could not get into the sack together because my blue oval and climacteric chart together made me unpredictably and extraordinarily fruitful most of the month, and I did not wish to have his ugly children. The true reason was because all people were made up of colors. After my climacteric, once I took over the responsibility for my menstrual cycle, I became almost entirely blue. I watched Max carefully for a year and realized that he was decidedly red. He often masqueraded as green, eating leafy vegetables or stuffing his pockets with foliage, but I detected his redness despite his efforts. He coated his cheeks with blue powder to hide their ruddiness, pretended to sulk rather than grow angry, and talked about the veins of the body rather than the blood. But I knew he was red, and there was no room for his redness in my body.

In typical Max-fashion, he left his response to my refusal to get into the sack with him under the upside down rinsing cup on my bathroom sink. There I found a little bottle of estrogen pills with the label: "Take three as directed by Max." Because Max believed that testosterone made up the earth's axis, he decided that estrogen made up the crust, and believed that excessive doses of it would make me desire to enfold him. He cut silhouettes of our bodies out of black construction paper to prove we had once been separated by plate tectonics.

So we argued:

The dowager's hump on the back of your neck, he insisted,

is the perfect size for my teeth, which will act to restrain rather to bite as I mount you suddenly from behind.

To retaliate, I showed him a picture of Arthur, the British television cat whose teeth were extracted to force him to eat cat food by dipping his paws in the can. Arthur, unlike Max, unwittingly ran a very successful campaign.

As a cat, Max persisted, I am designed to copulate up to eight times in twenty minutes, and you are denying me my sense of cat-self by refusing me your favors.

The female cat, I read from a book, viciously tears away from her mate as soon as he ejaculates.

Because, Max quoted, his seed is so fiery hot, that it almost burneth the female's place of conception.

Talk such as this always got Max excited, so I reminded him that the penis of the male cat was covered with reverse angled horny spines, and I did not, thank you, care to be ripped apart inside by his red presence.

Rejected, Max sulked for two weeks and left an index card in my panty drawer.

catamenia (kat uh-me ne-uh) *n. Your Personality.* The quality of being as nasty and changeable as a cat for no particular reason with monthly regularity.

I soothed Max by assuring him that he was not as ugly as I once thought. He basked in the compliment. The next morning I found another index card taped to the headboard of my bed.

catechist (kăt´uh-kist) *n.* The condition of having been kissed on the breast secretly by a cat (Max) while you slept unknowingly.

I stomped up the stairs and fidgeted out a clay replica of Max's body at my workbench, leaving off the head, hands, and feet. I dragged the severed cat paw he had given me down the back of his body, leaving deep gouges in the clay. Stabbing his groin with knitting needles, I chanted the spell I had prepared:

I poke thee,
I poke thee,
I toke the quell that's under the 'ee
Oh qualyway, oh qualyway,
Dash out the brains of Max I say.

Then I sewed his body into a sack with a replica of a live cat, as they used to do with adultresses, and threw it into a sink full of salty water.

I hated Max. I hated him because I relied on him. I never had to leave my house, because he brought me groceries and medicine and painted all my windows shut for me, calling me his Miss Havisham and Miss Emily Rosey and Mrs. Bates all rolled into one big lump. He encouraged me to become an entirely fictive character by bringing me old wedding cakes and dented pillows and taxidermy needles. He wrote novels starring me but never let me read them.

HERE IS A PLOT SUMMARY OF MY LATEST NOVEL© STARRING YOU
The Cat Queen

Freya (you), the Cat Queen, is holding her annual twelve-day slaughter of all flightless birds and large rodents. As is the custom, anyone in heat (you) can appear before the Cat Court and ask for a champion (Max). The fair cat Luna (you) rides into the court on a white ass, shrieking that her parents have been imprisoned in a pet taxi by a local veterinarian. The sturdy and athletic knight Ra (Max) gallantly offers to assist Luna (you). Despite the efforts of Duellona and Orptah (them), Ra and Luna (we) are betrothed and the veterinarian put to sleep. To everyone's surprise, Jesus (Max) appears suddenly and gives a cat to the widow Lorenza (you), which she uses to charm the Blatant Man, deformer of feline character and the last enemy of the Cat Court, and everyone returns to Freya's court (your bedroom) and frolics.

The basic plotline, he said, is, of course, plagiarized, but the story remains an allegory. As a joke, I offered Max a picture of a hairless cat which he could use as a self-portrait for the jacket flap of his novel. Predictably, Max did not get the joke, but was aroused by the attention I gave him.

Among the important and easily missed symbols in the novel, he said excitedly, is the Sistrum. The Sistrum is the ancient rattle which Ra carries into battle in his right paw.

Who cares? I said.

The blue oval at the top of the Sistrum, he said with a sneer, is the self-contained womb of your imagination, while the erect pillar of the handle stands for the corresponding male organ of Max, which enters the blue oval whenever it wishes.

Never, I insisted. No one enters my oval but me.

Then Max contorted his face and hissed wildly at me, slapping my face and throwing me onto the bed. He covered my knees with his and squeezed my wrists between his claws. His fingertips probed my lungs and strangled my circulation, cutting my oxygen into tiny gasps. He mashed his forehead into my chest and his drunken eyes seared their way down into my oval. Somehow, he covered it with a plunger and thrust the stick handle through the mouth, swindling out my deepest secrets without depositing anything intimate of his own. Somehow, I allowed him to walk his stained lips over my breasts, chewing his way through the very skin which preserved me.

Don't worry, he said, sucking away at me, all cats close their eyes while drinking milk.

I squeezed my eyes shut and tried to concentrate on my oval. This time, no soft teeth greeted my finger, but a pool of viscous lubricant bubbled with hate at my intrusion. I frantically searched deep into the grease and tried to find something with substance, but the only thing left was a fistful of raw wool.

Meanwhile, Max rubbed his toadstool penis over my opening, promising that he was no longer a cat, but a folklore, a literature, an occupation, a jukebox, a manufacturer, a rite-of-passage, a safe-deposit box, a savior, a religion, a chronicle of human manhood who would fill me with his bloodshot.

He forced his way into me, squeezing away whatever porosity was left in my bones. The schoolchildren flooded my yard in the moonlight, tapping a blue balloon into the air with their soft hands while I watched helplessly from behind the window. My climacteric chart tore itself into little bits, fluttering down the basement steps in an effort to seek the earth. The clay on my workbench rolled itself into a cavernous mouth, laughing and threatening to swallow me whole if I unclenched myself. And Max inflated and buried his hips into me again and again, as I pounded on his ribs with my fists, my throat retching with the taste of his redness.

A DIFFERENT LETTER

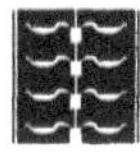

The Ground Hog (August 28, 1980)

I first met John Nibbs near the ground hog hole in the cemetery. He was jogging frantically around a headstone, slapping his knees with his palms and puffing grief with his chin. Never had I witnessed such discipline coupled with misery. Overwhelmed with compassion I rushed forward with a ready handshake and heartfelt condolences.

"Close friends?"

"No, we never met!" he sobbed, increasing his pace and bobbing his head from side to side.

The headstone read:

Here lies Manford Tussey,
Professor of Science at Juniata College for 29 years,
loving father and husband,
who died at 80 of natural causes.
1900-1980

"Isn't it tragic?" John said.

Then he stopped, sweating, and jotted something down on a small white pad.

Juniata College (1876-?)

From 1978 to 1981, John and I attended Juniata College, properly pronounce Won-eat-ah Cawl-edge, in Huntingdon, Pennsylvania. Juniata is an Indian name, meaning Great Fern. In 1826, the American Indian Neemomanish, a forward-thinking individual, stood his staunch figure on a hilltop, now known as the corner of Moore Street and Eighteenth Street, drove his spear into the spongy earth, and declared that he would build a school for the young of his tribe. Fifty years later, this school became Juniata College, which grew from a handful of teepees and mud-shacks into the present twenty-two concrete and brick structures, including the recently completed Binder Natatorium.

Juniata College is a highly respected liberal arts school offering training for young men and women in the business of living, through over fifty different undergraduate degree majors. Yet there's somehow a human quality to Juniata as well. During your visit, don't be surprised if a professor greets you and chats over tea and cakes in the impressive dining hall, the Baker Refectory, which offers a three-week cycle menu (see handbook), located in Ellis Hall. Then you might stroll along through the hallowed halls of the Cloister, or listen to the sound of the chimes from the historic Founder's Bell Tower. Other buildings trumpeting Juniata fame include the Pink Palace, the Brumbaugh Science Center, and Toad Hall. Be sure to take along any of our brochures for your friends as well, and drive home safely.

2170 Moore Street (September 7, 1980)

Moore Street, in Huntingdon, Pennsylvania, splits at Marjorie Heffelfinger's house. Moore Street East winds in an S curve past the IGA, takes a sharp left orbital turn at the third red light, and whips around the J. C. Blair Memorial Hospital. Then the gravitational pull joins it with Moore Street West, zooming past Juniata College and meeting itself again in front of Marjorie Heffelfinger's house at 2170 Moore Street.

John moved into Marjorie's house as a tenant on September 6, 1980.

"Marjorie Heffelfinger, meet Joe Schall," John said.

"How do you do?" I said.

"Yes," Marjorie said.

Marjorie's hair never moved. The wind could not disturb it because Marjorie never opened any windows. It was not like a sixty-three year old wire brush, because it had no plastic handle attached. It was not like a scouring pad, because you could not hold it in one hand and clean off the counter with it. It was not like a bristly, mesh, agrarian, convoluted, iron-grey, infested fortress because no words could describe it. It just sat there, seemingly pinned in place to an overstuffed green chair, never moving, refusing to be combed or comprehended. When Marjorie stood up, the entire mound of hair remained in place on the back of the chair.

John and I went into Marjorie's kitchen and stared. I was flabbergasted. Normally when I am flabbergasted, I picture a pair of huge Rolling-Stone-like lips flapping up and down in slow, wet disbelief. But not this time. I just stared, flabbergasted.

"Her husband died a year ago," John explained.

"In the kitchen?"

"Her son joined the service six months ago and married a Korean," John said.

"A gook," Marjorie yelled from the chair. "A gook he married and left me here alone to die."

With her dusty slippers, Marjorie had padded a fairly accurate representation of a right triangle around the kitchen. The base extended from the doorway to the refrigerator; the hypotenuse had endpoints at the refrigerator and sink; the side ran from the sink back to the doorway where John and I stood. The base was defined by bits of broccoli, mushrooms, hamburger, torn boxes of Weight Watcher's dinners, empty Cool Whip containers, tubs of Wispride cheese turned green, and fuzzy sections of Sunbean bread torn apart as if ready for the turkey. The hypotenuse was surrounded by Silverstone pans, pots caked with grease and rice, dirty dishes, spatulas and spoons, empty foil and plastic wrap rolls, crunched-up Keebler crackers, ice cream boxes in all the colors of the rainbow, and an unraveled ball of red yarn. The side of the triangle was lined with Glamour Kitty litter, broken glass, sheets of Bounce, slimy cat toys, cans of assorted Campbell's soups, a tub of margarine, and dirty laundry.

John and I stood at the apex of the triangle, appalled not at the knee-high accumulation of Marjorie's loneliness, not at her indifference to the filth she lived among, not at the shreds of twenty dollar bills sprinkled on the counter, but at the majestic clean inside of the triangle. The linoleum inside glared up at us, sparkling and speckless, as if licked clean by the sandpaper tongue of a giant cat who had studied geometry.

John jotted something down on a small white pad and we cleaned for two days.

Huntingdon, Pennsylvania (1749-?)

Huntingdon proudly houses Juniata College, and is also the County seat. Huntingdon is famous for its one-way streets. The fine for driving the wrong way down a one-way street in Huntingdon is $52, but visitors should not get the idea that Huntingdon is unfriendly to tourists. In fact, the folks at the Huntingtown Tourism Center will be happy to help lend an historical perspective to your visit. The Huntingtown Tourism Center is conveniently located at 612 Arch Street, which is a two-way street just three blocks from the railroad. The number to call is (814) 648-4440. Be sure not to miss Guy's Tourist Home, 614 Arch Street, located just a few convenient steps from the Huntingtown Tourism Center, which stands on the oldest foundation of any home in Huntingdon, dating back to 1799 according to popular legend. You can reach Guy's by phone between 8:00 and 12:00 and 1:00 and 3:00 Monday through Thursday, at (814) 648-0444, but why not stop in for a visit personally? Last year Huntingdon Borough Council reported that $2,192 was brought into the community because of the tourist trade. Top on the list of moneymaking tourist attractions was the former home of Marjorie Heffelfinger.

His Commitment (October 31, 1980)

"One day, Joe," John told me, "I will be committed."

"To where?"

"Nay sir, 'To what?' you must ask," he said.

"Why?" I said.

"To writing," he said. "That will be my commitment. To write. To experience emotional disaster and then write it down. To throttle myself to the edge of perception and fold the flap over to the other side. To boldly write as no man has written before."

So he searched his environment for new topics. Huntingdon had trains passing through it every forty-five minutes, so John said he would write a story about trains. He had a great interest in them, but only as symbols. Trains were something that might cut across your path at any time with a taunting whistle and without due warning, forcing you to slam on the brakes. He firmly believed that if all the trains in the world ran at the same time, the earth would split in two. I assured him that they would never organize, but he was committed to stop them. He stood on the tracks at 6:45 p.m., wearing a catcher's mask, his feet planted firmly and his right arm extended, poised to receive the 6:32 Amtrak.

When the train was a few feet away, he calmly stepped off the tracks and waved to the engineer, keeping his arm stretched in a salute until the train was out of sight. Then he wistfully added the experience to his list of potential story ideas on the small white pad. He called this list "The List."

His First Story (August 9, 1974)

"Life with Father"

by John Nibbs

I can't hide it anymore, I said. Father, I'm a teenage paranoid!

Then I waited a minute. My Father, who was a generous man, waited two minutes. Then he spoke to me for the first time in weeks.

Son, he said (for he was being affectionate), Son, he said—as he looked in the mirror—Son paranoia is a matter of perspective.

Whose, I said.

Theirs, he said.

Not mine, I said.

Theirs, he said.

But *I'm* the one who's paranoid, I said.

So are they, he said.

I was astounded. I realized that Father must have discovered some truth through his experiences. Perhaps Father held all of knowledge in his hand, perhaps he was a philosopher prophet, perhaps he was a spokesman for the whole human race, perhaps paranoia was a condition of our times, perhaps

But, I said.

Don't fight it, he said.

When, I said.

Now, he said.

And, I said.

You said it, he said.

But that means all of my efforts are futile, I said. That means something beyond words. That means we're all just a bunch of teenage paranoids running around interrupting ourselves spouting unfinished clichés about life like, like

If the shoe fits, he said.

Mrs. Nibbs (December 28, 1980)

When I visited over Christmas break, his mother fed me well, determined to "nurse me back to health." At breakfast, I slipped my fourth helping of blueberry pancakes to the dog, because the garlic was making me sick. She worked garlic into every meal because it was "the great healer." At lunch I choked on the garlic in the tomato soup, which convinced her that my feedings were not frequent enough. At supper Mrs. Nibbs spoke to John.

"Buster," she said, "tomorrow you're going to get a haircut or else start wearing a hairnet. Your hair is falling in Joe's food."

John didn't look up from his writing, but continued to dutifully sip his soup.

His mother melted all over the driveway when I left. I was "the son she never had."

His First Lay (July 25, 1976)

"Locomotion"
by John Nibbs

I remember my first driving experience.

My sex-ed teacher was in the back seat taking notes.

My father was in the front seat coaching me.

"Is this the first time you've been behind the wheel, or did one of your sisters take you up to the school parking lot?" father asked.

My sex-ed teacher snickered and slid down lower in her seat. At first I resented her insinuations, but I, and she, knew they were well-founded.

"No . . . my first time," I said nervously.

Even now when I am driving it is sometimes as if my father is sitting beside me—his head turned towards me with an ambiguous smile on his face. As I catch a sideways glimpse of that smile I'm unsure whether he is about to praise my performance or unfasten my seat belt.

It is not as I had imagined. Anticipation leaks out more quickly than enjoyment is understood. There is fear here. I did not expect that.

I try not to think about what I'm doing so much. Father senses my thought.

"Don't worry so much about technique. Just try to concentrate," he says, "and relax."

"Good advice for a virgin," my sex-ed teacher says.

"It will help if you keep quiet," I mutter under my breath, and she chuckles, thinking that I am talking to father.

The white lines flicker by with increasing speed despite

my unchanging rhythm. I look to my left side and the guard rails flow together in a watery blur; I look to the horizon ahead and see my sex-ed teaching bobbing up and down on the ocean waves. I am sensitive to my vulnerability, but it occurs to me that I also have great power with a simple touch of my hand. For the moment I feel like I will never tire of this.

"If only one could always feel so innocent about it . . ." my sex-ed teacher says from the rearview mirror.

To this day I am plagued by back-seat drivers.

When we were finished, I stepped out of the car and placed my feet firmly on the macadam, but my body remained in a swaying euphoria for a moment.

"Was it a letdown for you?" father asked.

"I don't know . . ." I said strangely. "It's like, I can't describe it; it's nice but the reality and the romance together just, just don't . . ."

"I understand," dad said, his hand on my shaking shoulder.

Senior Value Studies (May 1, 1981)

At Juniata College, everyone was required to take "Senior Value Studies," a pass/fail course designed to enhance your value touchstones and general living skills one last time before graduation.

The question on our final was:

> *Examine the moral implications of Voluntary*
> *Euthanasia, using both logical and ethical reasoning.*
> *You have three hours.*

John wrote:

> *If someone is a vegetable, it is fruitless to try*
> *to keep him alive on a machine.*

He got an A.

My First Lay (May 2, 1981)

King Queen was the resident assistant for the second floor of Tussey-Terrace dormitory at Juniata College. John claimed that she never slept, but hummed about busily all night watching the hive. He also claimed that despite her enormous size, she spent much of her time invisible. This, he said, was why one rarely saw her, but heard stories about her simply showing up somewhere uninvited all the time.

I met King Queen when she was not invisible. As I walked to the silverware dispenser in the Baker Refectory, I noticed people were looking my way quizzically. Instinctively, I turned my head to find John walking just a few inches away, dragging his feet, bobbing his head up and down with his tongue hanging out, and shaking his arms spastically, as I walked along in my normal state with sensible shoes, a straight back, and a flushed face. I whispered to John to stop it, but he continued doggedly on with contorted enthusiasm, convinced that the rest of the world was walking off-key.

I bumped into something spongy with my tray, my silverware clattering to the floor. I gulped and looked straight up into King Queen's pneumatic face. She smiled. She had one silver tooth and halitosis.

"H . . . Hi," I stammered.

"Hehe, fancy bumping into you like this," John drooled from behind my back.

I tried to elbow him, spilling both glasses of milk onto my tray, but I didn't dare look away from her smiling face, even though milk was seeping into my double-knit pants leg.

"Excuse me," she said with a deep, flirtatious rasp, tipping my tray with her gut as she exhaled all over me.

"Why? You haven't done anything yet," John said from behind me.

"No, excuse *me,*" I insisted, milk filling my right shoe.

I set my tray down on the nearest table and limped out of the Baker Refectory with as much dignity as possible, with John still following spastically as if nothing had happened.

I didn't know what to say, but was fascinated at the quiet circles of milk trailing behind me.

John whipped out his small white pad and added something to "The List."

The List (May 24, 1981)

by John Nibbs

Stories to work on

— the time that Joe and I gave CPR to the cat (successfully?) and Joe wrote a letter to the *Juniatian* proposing that an anatomic feline should be included in all CPR classes

— the time Joe and I met jogging in the cemetery and he tripped in the ground hog hole

— write a story in reverse in which it is just as sensible when read backwards (work on syntax here and transitions from back to front)

— the time Joe helped clean up Marjorie's kitchen and broke stacks of plates so he wouldn't have to wash them

— when Marjorie came up to my bedroom and sat on my bed and touched my knee and asked me if I ever got lonely (hard to have fun with this one, maybe not enough distance but could be fun in a gross way—p.p. purple skin blotches focus)

— when Joe argued in Psych 101 class that positive reinforcement for mutes could be listening to tapes of any sounds they made (don't scrap the bowel movement idea after all)

— Joe sent himself a sympathy card

— about the time I tried to stop the train and Joe called the police

— Joe's quantum theory of humanity (about defining observed systems by forcing them into isolation but systems always seeking isolation in order to avoid definition idea)

— when King Queen met Joe and spilled milk all over him/her (write as though it's a wet dream)

— a self-conscious (pedantic?) circular story in first person about a *different* writer using stories written by ***him*** and blaming all flaws on him (somewhere call this technique a Freudian slipper for the critics to walk around in)

— the time Joe left a copy of *V.* on Dick Graves' desk (name significance? could do something with Dick's penchant for scatalogical literary humor here) on Shakespeare's birthday (a few will get it)

— don't save any stories to tell

A Letter (July 3, 1988)

Marjorie Heffelfinger
2170 Moore Street
Huntingdon, Pa.
16652

John Nibbs
Po Box 1321
Star route
Seward, Alaska

Dear John:
I got your address from Joe. He didn't know the zipcode.
I hope you don't mind. I hope this
get's to you OK. I hope your not still mad at me. I know you

were right I always am an alcoholic. I am writing to you to return
your money to you and tell you that I am dying soon of hip cancer.
I am not sure how much longer I will live so I am glad I am doing
this while I am still clear in my head. I am sending you back 900
dollars which is how much rent money you payed when you live here.
I think you deserve back your money because Joe told me that you need
it bad and I dont and you deserve it you helped me so much with keeping me happy for a while in my life and I really do greatly appreciate
it so much. I know you are busy and far away at all but I hope you could come
back for my funeral sometimes Joe said he would contact you about
it and maybe you would be willing to give me my ulogy at the funeral.

With love and respect,
Marjorie Heffelfinger.

A Different Letter (August 19, 1992)

dear joe

am stasrting a new fad as you probaly already noticed.haven't ev even been typing for twolines sand i havealready discovered why e.e. cummings never usex capital letters he was too lazy and profund. so am i. the deal here is that i'm tired go wriiting

fiction and i will write you fact for awhile. i will even be including mistakes in typing just to show you i'm mortal i thought i'd let you in on that secret. strange th thing being mortal it is a bit like being let in on a secret partial but not the whole thing. like someone sneaking behind you and saying "i now (n0) know a girl who likes you" and then leaving you to ponder such immortal questions as who.why, and is she pretty? immortality has driven some men to greatness and othe ers to insanity. just to look at full moon hovering luminously in the late summers sky causes the most simple man to ponder on the age and the history of that dead star then finally to measure his own brief existence against the other's. Chills of dread, or is it futility, run up the spine as the mortal's time line measures up woefully short to the moon's. we are tyuna left to rage bitterly at the lunar betrayer or lover and weepsilently; whatever is our want.; we are not what we once were anymore are we joe? our father's gone our children to come, the future of our earthly garden, the last mushroom cloud—time is the final frontier.
have i got a story to tell you,.
we went to this banquet os saturday at some country lub . .it was in honor of the graduating nurses of which ron's sister laurie was one. After an hour I got significantly buzzed enough to hold out my marischino cherry to ron in front of his whole family and ask him if I should notify the lost and found department. then we went to this place called the peanut barn.d
well i was tsadning admiring the bartender who was a pretty thing named cathy. charley told me i should 'scoop up on her" because she was pretty and could probably cook fairly well. well like what was i supposed to do jest run over there an sweep here of her feet and tell her i like my steaks rare and my women sunnysideup? instead i ending up talking to laurie ie on one side of me and welllll i'.

hanging around and sucking some brews and getting a little cuddley with laurie and although she has a slightly homey face telling her a story about marjorie to the tune of "iswear that there were seven half gallons of vodka in her room all empty mind you and she jult lay there naked and warty with one breast flopped over the side of the bed and dangling about an inch off the floor. she just lay there with her eyes rolled back in her head anmd filled the room with purple curses. an d just when i started to get upset and into it all of the sudden this somewhat chubby blonde girl knocks rons coat on the floor. i asked her if she did it on purpose to which she relpied in the affirmative "yeah what the fucks 'sit to you?" taken aback i said it would have been sporting of her to put the coat anywhere but on the beer sotten floor / ron jumped in and said "listen bitch if you want to talk like that i'm gonnaknock you right on your ass.understand?" turning to me he sid that that wsa how you had to talk to drunken bar sluts like her. she stsrted punching ron and i pummeled her into a sack of tears by saying "you're just a woman" over and over again in varying tones of disgust, she was then dragged away by her apologetic friends then she passed out and was raped by an appreci apprjtrevcio atei c appreciateive gang of motorcyle hoodlums.
i must get to bed. it's very late and drunken i'll send off toy oyou a real story soon.

John

A Real Story (September 28, 1992)

"The Process"

by John Nibbs

But I was worried that I'd never finish, and I didn't think that she would help me. But let me start over again.

So the goal was to finish, you understand, to simply finish my train of thought without dying. Sure, I told her, anyone can stop thinking by dying, but it's the great man who stops his train of thought and lives. And when I told her about my project I thought she would laugh at me, but she just asked how she could help me.

But I haven't told you enough about it yet for you to truly understand my condition. I was trying not just to stop my thinking but to let my train of thought run its complete course. I was trying to reach the perfect zero of unthought, when my mind would become naturally static and my train of thought disappear. I realize that this was hard for you to understand, for this is my own unique thought which I am constructing through a long and sometimes painful process. I see that I just slipped out of the past tense and into the present. However, I will not change this because I want you to understand that this is part of my condition too. Fortunately I have discovered that my past thoughts are revocable and my present thoughts will soon be past. This, the new mindblowing thought all my own, is what helped inspire me to conduct my process. To make my thoughts stop. To end my thoughts completely instead of letting one run into another without interrupting . . . in short, to have a complete thought, then stop.[1]

But how, she asked me, and at this point I think you may be ready to ask the same question. But first you may be wondering about the long and sometimes painful process involved in arriving at this great thought of mine. You see, I used to think that I was a common man with common thoughts, because I did not have a job and because everyone always told me I was common. As I'm sure even you can imagine, this made

[1](without dying, remember)

me feel incredibly common. So I thought for many hours about how to become truly great, then one day I had an astounding thought all my own, and through it I discovered the key to greatness. This thought is one which would, or will, deliver all men from anguish. I will not tell you what this astounding thought is however, for I have forgotten it. Now if you think it is a sign of weakness in me to have forgotten this thought then you should know that I did not lose this thought by accident as any common man could, but purposely erased it from my memory to prove my strength. Remember that you do not know exactly what this astounding thought is, and neither do I, but I do recall that this thought is what inspired my thought to completely stop my train of thought. I realize that this is hard for you to grasp. Since you are confused by now, I will speak plainer: logically, this astounding thought was not unlike my thought of completely stopping my thinking, or it would not have been significant enough to forget.

And now you know my complete state of mind, and I think you are ready to understand my process. But I still wonder why *she* helped with my process when I never told her about its history—of how I rose above the common man by starting my process by forgetting my astounding thought. I never told her. And I thought about why she was helping me a lot until I realized that I might just keep on thinking about it without finding the answer so I stopped thinking that thought since to stop thinking completely was my goal. And so I was one step closer to my goal by eliminating that thought, and even though I'm telling you about it now for your illumination, I still am being careful not to think about it.

But the real story here lies within the process of completing my train of thought. Naturally I didn't want to think too hard about how to go about this business because that would defeat my purpose, so when I told her this she suggested we experiment. Without thinking about it, I agreed instantly. You should know by now that I was just secretly playing her game for amusement, plus I am beginning to dislike her so I humor her a little. We began her first experiment which was simply to have a long conversation with each other until hopefully I would become so involved in talking that I would stop thinking altogether. I cannot remember any of this conversation, which is a good sign, but I do remember that it made me sick in the toilet. She said then that this conversation was very revealing which shows she does not truly understand what my process is all about. Of course, I can understand why she cannot understand for she is common but claims to be a great doctor. I know from experience that common people often believe falsely that they are truly great. And when I finish my process and end all my thought these types of people will all look up to me as a great philosopher or something.

I forget what our second conversation was about except that I remember telling her she was starting to make me think about the past and that's what I've got to stop doing thinking. And damn her, damn her who I hate now she doesn't help me a bit, she said the story I told her about my father which also made me sick in the toilet was very revealing which shows she is a fool who doesn't realize that it is a story about nothing and maybe it never even happened and I just made it up in fact the more I think about it which I am trying not to do the more I think I never even *had* a father and maybe my thoughts are just making me think I had one to keep me from my process but I will show them and her and I told her and grabbed her and they grabbed me and dragged her away from me and put me in a private room so I could try to not think on my own.

And now I think I will begin.

WIDE ARCS AND S CURVES

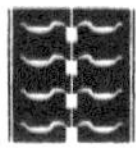

Part 1—Background

For a long while Thomas's mind was completely occupied by whatever scrapbook sat on the desk in front of him, and he read by the light of a yellow bulb, uninterrupted by his usual daydreams about sharply angled anorexic women and the world's fastest printing press. Occasionally he fell asleep and woke up a few hours later with his nose clamped between the opened pages of a scrapbook, a spittle stain spread over some of the articles. When this had first happened, he decided that his nose and forehead were always a bit too rounded anyway, and he began to prefer sleeping with this face rested against the worn newspaper clippings. Gradually, he thought of his face as an overread, wrinkled newspaper. Sometimes he woke with crisscrossing patterns of printer's ink splotched over his cheeks.

The scrapbooks had come along just when he needed them—six months after he had lost his job as the "Street Smarter" reporter for *The Metro.* He had been forced to forfeit both the job and the pen name of Charlie Spikes, which the paper had routinely assigned him.

"Sorry Spikes," Editor Bradley said, handing him a letter of dismissal. "Your style is just too damned romantic. We need information, not ideals. Go write a novel or get married or something."

But, even with the job gone, Thomas couldn't shrug off the habits he'd acquired during his two years of writing a weekly column on what he called "New York's Finest Street People." He continued to huddle next to burner barrels and take notes, his notebook hidden within his raincoat as though he were still doing clandestine research for his column. To establish his credibility with the street people, he exploited all the usual tricks of the trade. He strapped old pillows underneath his clothes with bungie cords so that, as he sat in front of the Carson and Lundin building, he appeared to have folds of fat hanging from his body. When he wiggled a bit on his stool, the coins from his tin cup spilled onto his lap and he made a show of digging them from between the tight crevices of his trousers. He practiced looking at his face in the passenger windows of moving cars. He looked like the young Albert Einstein without the moustache. The same perpetually raised eyebrows, hourglass ears covered by unnaturally windblown and brittle hair, a chin which eventually met the downturned corners of the mouth in intelligent, abstract harmony, and, in the center of it all, a nose which was not content until it drooped outward into cheeks, then flattened suddenly and seemed to slide off his face. As the cars flashed by, he changed his countenance during the lulls between the passenger windows, hoping that passers-by would notice his face and think him spastic.

Other techniques were designed to arouse even more sympathy. Some days he pretended to be blind, bumping into people indiscreetly and carrying a sign which said "Pardon my lack of sight. At my last job I put balls and jacks in bags and filled plastic eggs with Silly Putty. I did not write this." He used names like Rockwin, Boochy, Mal, and Elfin to fit in with the other street people, but he sensed that they still doubted his authenticity, and carried a new cardboard sign: "Marx was right about Capitalism. Wrong about God. (Come join me—normal people only)." He didn't know what the sign meant, but he knew he believed in God and did not believe in Marx. He had copied most of the sign from a wall on East Ninth Street, and it seemed to make some of the street people more respectful. They began to share their scraps of food from the trash cans, and one of them offered Thomas a "protection service" if he gave him a cut of his daily profits.

But he still didn't feel he was one of them. He tried to feel downtrodden and wildly eccentric, but he found himself plagued by, as Editor Bradley had called it, his romantic idealism. No matter how pitiful the street people he imitated were, he couldn't help but imagine them strolling down Fifth Avenue in fashionable skirts or three-piece suits, carrying briefcases, umbrellas, folded newspapers, and loaves of French bread, then dining with all the proper utensils in heated or air-conditioned rooms. He strolled down Fifth Avenue himself for a while, using an irregular rolling limp he had learned from a fat man, which was mostly a selective thrust and half-turn of the hip joint. He loaded the right-hand pocket of his army jacket with pebbles to enhance the effect, and the shreds of his dull green trousers hung like mini-stalactites from his waist, flapping around his exposed, skinny calves. Sockless, he wore the traditional heavy black boots with no laces and shriveled tongues, and, at night, left them upside down under the radiator in his apartment to keep them stiff.

Finally, he decided that if he truly wanted to become one of them, he would have to forsake the very comforts which he liked to imagine them having. So he got evicted from his apartment by refusing to pay his rent for two months in a row, sending his landlord an envelope full of crushed cockroaches instead.

He took a vow of silence and waited for something important to happen. His reporter's instincts drew him to hold a stare-down with the painted and wall-papered windows of an abandoned building, as he tried to decide if the "Condemned" sign in front of it was authentic or Editor Bradley's twisted idea of a snipe hunt lying in wait for him. He imagined himself breaking into the building in search of an interesting story, with all of his old colleagues bursting from behind the woodwork, yelling "Snipe! Snipe! Snipe!" then handing him a trophy of a jackalope and having a big party to celebrate his dismissal. But when no one entered or exited the building for two days, he grew less suspicious, and decided to claim it as his own. He pulled the sign from the lawn, broke a basement window with it, and crawled onto a long ledge just a foot below the window. He turned around on all fours in the tiny space, then shoved the sign into place over the broken glass, turning its "Condemned" message out to the rest of the world, and sealing himself into complete darkness. He shuffled around again on his hands and knees, then took four crawls forward in the dark, until his hands failed to find the floor and his body sprawled flat. Headfirst, he slid down the metal incline of a coal chute and landed safely in a pile of books. Trying to sit up straight, he knocked the back of his head against the ceiling, then groped around with his hands and accidentally found a light bulb chain. His face and arms sprinkled with coal dust, he turned on a yellow light bulb, illuminating the once-whitewashed walls of a huge coal bin. He found himself sitting on a collection of scrapbooks piled four feet high.

He could feel that his face bled from several cuts, and he enjoyed the notion that he had been suddenly and arbitrarily battered. His most recent cut, he remembered, had been from the sharp edge of a piece of paper Editor Bradley had unexpectedly yanked from his hands. He held up his hands and inspected the backs of them under the yellow bulb. His wrists reminded him of left-over chicken bones, branching off into ghostly blue rivulets which were interrupted by occasional hairs. Every alternate finger boasted a scar. One from a girl's shoe-buckle when he was nine; one from a broken test tube in seventh grade; one from a cat that refused to eat from his palm; one from a piece of twine he had wrapped too tightly and left on for two hours in the newspaper office. He once showed Editor Bradley each of his scars, describing each one as another notch in his ladder of maturity. Meanwhile the editor's own white fingers flickered over the typewriter keys, composing a note for Thomas which informed him that a hand was the terminal part of the human arm below the wrist, structured from a palm, four fingers, and an opposable thumb, and he should, thank you, just get the hell back to work. Thomas let out a convincing ironic smile and put his hand on the cracked surface of one of the scrapbooks underneath him, unsure whether he was about to detonate or caress it.

Thus began his adventure with the scrapbooks. As he crawled out of the coal bin to explore the rest of the basement, he took full stock of his good fortune: he had no job or other obligations, no landlord bothering him for a check, no family looking for him, less than one-hundred dollars to carry around, a rent-free basement of his own, which included a water heater, an oil burner, a toolbox, assorted articles of broken furniture, and a set of summer screens—plus a coal bin full of scrapbooks, which probably housed thousands of possibilities for a willing, long-subdued imagination.

He never knew that the scrapbooks had been left in the coal bin by Cyril Sanders, who lived on the first floor. Cyril had relatives in London who sent him the three newspapers he considered most representative of the world—*The Guardian, The Daily Express,* and *The Sun*—and he had spent twenty-two years assembling the scrapbooks from the most interesting articles he could find in the newspapers. Then, knowing he would soon die, he piled the scrapbooks in the coal bin, staked the "Condemned" sign in his front lawn, and nailed all the doors shut from the inside. He spent the remaining three days of his life hulked over his journals for hours at a time and wrote love poems to Emily Dickinson. He hoped to die with his pen still in his hand, trailing ink across the page, a faded white rose in his shirt pocket. Cyril imagined the climactic scene: someday the neighbors would complain about a stink, the police would come to pry open the front door, and they would all marvel when they found his board-like, rotted body slumped forward over his poetry. The next day's issue of *The Daily Express* would contain a romantic story of the mysterious man who had died alone but with dignity, after dedicating his later life to a forlorn love for Emily Dickinson and to the preservation of the world's most fascinating items of news. He was sure they would find the scrapbooks in the coal bin and print photographs of them on page one of every major newspaper in the world.

Thomas, unaware of the living melodrama upstairs, crawled nostalgically up the chute and through the window, and bravely stalked back onto the streets to prepare for his new life. He imagined himself to be a once-successful accountant who had just lost his job after a stock market crash. Pure and brutal survival was the natural order, and he set his mouth accordingly. With his teeth he tore the collar button from his army jacket, then shoved his hand inside and yanked on the underarm of his T-shirt until it tore. He stole a burlap sack from a woman as she slept under a fire escape and used it to wipe the dried blood from the cuts on his face. He filled the bloody sack with armloads of canned goods taken from a "Cans For CROP" box sitting on some church steps, and stuffed his pockets with a clothesline of clean diapers that a pregnant woman in pink curlers had hung that morning. Finally, he secured toilet- and drinking-water facilities by breaking the lock on the bathroom door of the gas station across the street from his basement, and tapped loose all the hinge pins with stones in case they fixed the lock.

Thomas began to perceive that the city of New York had been built for his convenience. He had the feeling that everything that had happened since he lost his job had been designed to lead him through the front door of a *Job Lot Trading Company* to make some important purchases. He sensed that whatever he bought in the store would some day make up the critical scene in the historical movie about his life. While the other customers stared at his blackened and overstuffed clothing, he bought a can opener and a packet of ten pens and four notebooks in which to record his upcoming reminiscences. History, he knew, was about to be very competently made. On the way home, he wrote "My Various Memoirs" on page one of each of the notebooks.

"I will no longer concern myself with the world of wristwatches," he wrote in the first notebook, and dropped his Timex into the sewer.

Back in the basement, he measured his days and nights by each pull of the light bulb chain in the coal bin. If the yellow bulb was on, Thomas called it day. He turned on the three white bulbs in the living room section of the basement only to see his home better, and they did not affect the length of his days. The burlap sack he had stolen became the bed on which he slept, with an underpad made from some copies of *The Metro* which he had found in a garbage can. He positioned the bed so that his eyes focused on the yellow bulb as soon as he woke up.

For two of Thomas's days, he wiped the coal dust from each scrapbook with the diapers, then stacked the cleaned books neatly in the south end of the living room, where he had built shelves from the summer screens and the backs of dining room chairs. Then, as he counted the articles meticulously, he wrote a number on the side of each book which corresponded to the number of articles it contained, and thereby gave each book a personality. This new job had rekindled his interest in numerology, and he now had the freedom to let it be the controlling force of his life once again. He recalled the days when he had written for the paper and had aspired to become a professional numerologist.

Two years earlier, as he read a book on numerology, Thomas had been moved by E. T. Bell's struggle of trying to numerologize his name into 666. Bell had tried it in English, French, German, Italian, Dutch, Russian, Latin, Greek, Chinese, Sanskrit, and Hebrew, but the closest he got was 66 and 6666. Bell had been devastated by his failure, since any ordinary man's name was supposed to numerologize into 666, but Thomas believed that Bell's failure made him extraordinary, and he emulated the passion which had driven Bell to depression. Thomas changed his last name spontaneously, and from that moment became Thomas Bell. When he closed Bell's book, he stared for a long time into a hand mirror, and impulsively expanded on the Friendship Philosophy of Pythagoras that he had just read about:

"A true friend," he said, after setting his jaw squarely in imitation of Pythagoras, "is merely another I. Henceforth I shall embrace the theory that all people who share amicable numbers with me are my friends."

Thomas then began to think of people in terms of their proper divisors and sums, and he made a habit of intuiting which strangers shared amicable numbers with him as he walked to work each morning. He tipped his hat to them brightly as they passed by.

One day, while writing one of his columns for *The Metro,* he decided that 4 was the most perfect number. He figured out how the hour, day, month, year, and his body were all divided into 4 cyclic parts. In Sunday School, the nuns had told him that the Holy Trinity was incomplete unless a fourth party prayed to it. He remembered that his father used to hit him across the back with the strap in multiples of 4, and the street people's peak hour was 4 p.m. Editor Bradley threatened to fire him if he continued to write about how all street people lived in a fourth dimension beyond the capacity of ordinary minds.

So Thomas had abandoned his faith in numerology in print, but in private he still held a passion for it. In his basement, there was no public outcry to disturb him, so he named each scrapbook with the appropriate number and even declared number 60 to be secretly married to one of the other scrapbooks, since, when raised to the fourth power, it equaled Plato's famous nuptial number of 12,960,000. He would not be surprised, therefore, when he found that 4 of the articles in number 60 were concerned with the mysterious and seemingly unconnected murders of recent brides.

He had no interest in the rest of the house. He never bothered to find out that the fourth wooden step on the stairway up to the first floor would have probably broken under his weight. He never noticed the noise of the mouse chasing a walnut on top of his ceiling, nor the thump Cyril made as he wrote his last poem and fell sideways from his chair, dead. Thomas filled himself with other matters, delighting in having 4 prime numbers among his collection, two of them composites. After four of his days of work, he wrote in his notebook that he now owned 256 scrapbooks, which was 4 to the fourth power, and the 256 scrapbooks contained 65,536 articles exactly, which was 256 squared. Even before reading any of the articles, he filled his entire first notebook of memoirs with theorems, equations, approximations, and extrapolations.

The coal bin became the quiet room set aside for reading and writing, and after he had safely named and filed all his scrapbooks—his friends—he sat at the desk he had built under the yellow bulb and pondered his future.

"All my life," he wrote in his second notebook, "I have begun in doubt, ambled on to certitude, tripped over conviction, and throttled into oblivion with my thinning hair waving in the breeze. My romanticism and ideals swell within me, only to be trampled into the 42nd Street gutter by giant jungle elephants. But now my potential is unlimited. I am happy."

So Thomas paged through the scrapbooks unhurriedly and shook hands with the characters he liked, allowing his imagination to establish the rules of the game. He read his favorite articles four times exactly, first the usual way, then upside down, then with head cocked to the right, and finally with his hands covering the words and his eyes closed.

Part 2—Death

For twenty-two of Thomas's days, he read through the scrapbooks, until he came across something which fully sparked his imagination. It happened as he read from scrapbook 88—the number of eternity. He eagerly absorbed every word about the Holy Patch. According to the article, the Holy Patch was the only authentic remains of Christ's robe, which a woman named Tamar had woven for him after he repaired her loom. While Christ carried his cross-beam, the robe partially protected one shoulder from the whipping by Roman flagrums—lashes with leather tongs weighted by joined balls of lead or sheep vertebrae. The Romans had cast lots for the robe as Christ waited for death on the cross, and it was won by a centurion named Marcellus Gallio, who eventually became Christian and was executed by Caligula for publicly proclaiming his faith. Gallio handed the robe to his father just before he was killed, and now its memory had been passed on through the generations into Thomas's hands.

According to the article, the Holy Patch was the last remaining fragment of material from Christ's robe, and was in two pieces. In the eighteenth century, a Dominican Inquisitor had torn the Patch in two while testing it for elasticity. There was a rival patch, fully intact, at Grottoferrata in the Abruzzi, but Thomas concluded that it was an imposter when he read that it was not universally accepted. His conviction was that one should trust what appeared in print either passionately or not at all.

He found the story of the Holy Patch so compelling that he knew it was intended to change his life. The Patch was to become a personal symbol for him. Tentatively, Thomas decided to have a religious experience.

He closed his notebook and turned off the yellow bulb. With one pull of the chain, he became a successful New York journalist with an unlimited expense account, which made it easy for him to fly to Rome, buy a car, and drive to the Church of Saints Cornelius and Cyprian at Calcata, where the Patch was enshrined. His general plan was to steal the Patch and use it to find religion. He pretended to be featuring the Patch in an upcoming column for *The Metro,* and imagined that he broke into the church, drugged the main monk, and smashed the spherical reliquary with a crowbar, freeing the Patch from its brass, lead, gold, and crystal confinement.

Then he was faced with two immediate problems. The first was journalistic. Thomas knew that if he were to write "the Holy Patch" again and again in his memoirs, he would lose objectivity and become irreverent. So he needed an alias for it which was idiomatic but not sanctimonious, definitive yet masked, functional yet lofty, nostalgic yet unpretentious, emphatic but not overdone. Ideally, he thought, he needed a numerological riddle to represent it. Simply calling it "Patch-4" would have been too obvious, and since all the good sacred numbers were already taken, he would dupe the world by naming it with what he called a sight-cryptogram: a word-number riddle that was based on his two favorite senses—sight and math.

He thought about the Patch's appearance. To keep it waterproof and dust-free during their imaginary travels, he had scotch-taped its two halves together in his mind and inserted them into a 2-inch square of plastic, lining the edges with staples so that it was sealed securely and easily found in his pocket. Cupped in his hand it was a tiny bastion, a bargaining chip he could use to make Editor Bradley envious, a timeless toy that went "wuka, wuka, wuka" when he waved it in the pitch darkness of the coal bin.

He turned on the yellow bulb and drew a one-dimensional picture of the Patch in his notebook. It looked, he realized, like nothing more than an innocent piece of firm plastic. He wrote down the word "Plastic" and set it aside. Then he chose the word "firm," since it had four letters, as the key to his sight-cryptogram. "Firm" numerologized easily into 6, 9, 18, and 13, using the common English alphabet as the base. Then he exploited an old numerologist's trick: dividing the 6, 9, and 18 by 3, which left him with the ascending units, 2, 3, 6, and 13. Next he pulled the number-reordering device which he'd established as his trademark, multiplying the 2 by the 13 and the 3 by the 6, and adding together the results. Magically, he came up with the very number he'd had in mind from the start: 44. So, in Thomas's mind, the word "firm" now equalled 44. In his mind, he would only refer to the Holy Patch as 44.

His second immediate problem was the oily man. From the moment he had read about the Patch, he imagined that an oily man followed him with an earnest look on his face. The man's reflection could not be seen in a regular mirror, but Thomas noticed that if he used the Patch as a rear view mirror while pretending to walk down a busy Italian street, he could make out the oily man's basic shapes. There was usually something organic and shimmering about him. He had burly legs attached to a torso in the shape of half an upside down pentagon. He had a thick, possibly Turkish, moustache, and his forehead sloped unnaturally forward, which gave his profile a strange, but somehow familiar, re-entrant angle kind of look. His shoes were bulky and made of a fashionable fabric which looked heavy when wet—terrycloth as far as Thomas could tell. The unusual thing about him, though, was that he suavely carried a mask under his right arm. It looked like a catcher's mask, except it had steel handlebars on each side for easier removal and extra padding to accommodate his unnaturally sharp chin. Plus the man was decidedly oily, not motor oily but vegetable oily, and he slurped his way through the Italian crowds like an oblique cylinder of ice through a tube.

The oily man was a fairly good tracker, so Thomas thumbed through the scrapbook pages quickly and pretended to be a Vegas blackjack dealer, hoping to lose the man with his flashy sleight-of-hand. When this didn't seem to work, he imagined himself back in Italy again, where he turned corners sharply or ducked into alleys and up fire escapes, throwing the oily man off the scent for a time. But the man's geometric properties and general unctuousness allowed him to wrap his way around angled objects intimately, and Thomas found that he offered a more interesting challenge when he traveled in wide arcs and S curves. Always the oily man would reappear among the Italian crowds when Thomas least expected it, while he pretended to sit in a café or taxi and paged through the scrapbooks to plan his itinerary.

Just after a refreshing nap on the scrapbook in front of him, Thomas realized that a pattern of articles about undertakers from San Francisco had developed in his reading habits. He knew that if he were to have a religious experience, he would eventually have to face death, so he resolved to confront it by visiting some of the undertakers in California, which he had nicknamed the Land of the Dead.

Once in San Francisco, he planned a surprise visit to a firm of undertakers he had read about in scrapbook 100—the death number. He would stagger into their parlor with a pale look on his face, pretending to be a customer stricken with a terminal disease. They, in typical undertaker fashion, would roll away trolleys, turn off the radio, and straighten their ties.

Once, after Editor Bradley had accused him of being obsessed with death, Thomas had conducted a study of undertakers, and he understood them to be automatons in dark suits whose brains had been systematically rewired. Of course, he told himself, they were all necrophiles, who chuckled at the world's misconception that the worst thing they did was sleep with an occasional corpse. He imagined that, while still in puberty, they all attended a special school of necrophilia, where they were taught the diction of decay, the worship of technique, and the love of things with putrid smells which floated in quiet lakes. Speakers hidden in their pillows encouraged them to have dreams about clocks lodged in peoples' spines, painless dismemberment, and electric transformers pumping cold blood through high-tension cables. Their only passions were the propaganda and paraphernalia of death.

Thomas reviewed the notes he had taken from the scrapbooks on his favorite San Francisco undertakers. His attention lingered on the firm of Ody, Giles, and Washington, who he concluded were actually necrophilic triplets masquerading as business partners. For a while, he rooted his mind completely in their funeral parlor:

"Are you from San Francisco?"

Thomas nodded.

"Then you're in luck. You've read about our Christmas gift special in the newspaper, haven't you? Fine thing the newspaper. If you die on December 4th, 8th, 12th, 16th, 20th, 24th, or 28th, you get a free burial worth four thousand dollars."

Thomas realized that they were trying to woo him with their undertaker charms.

"How festive," he said, rapping on a coffin. "Is this one really solid copper like the sign says?"

"Yes," said Giles, stepping forward. "Notice how the side and top of the coffin are brushed to prove that it's solid. This one is likely to last a hundred years."

"Why should I be surrounded by copper when I'm dead?"

"John F. Kennedy was," Washington argued, shifting his weight onto the other foot, "but most people don't know that *inside* his copper casket were glass domes with steel locks that snapped shut and hermetically sealed him. A casket within a casket! Now why didn't that ever come out in the press?"

Thomas knew that Washington was secretly accusing him of being an unconscientious reporter, hoping to break his concentration and perhaps even make him one of their protégés. He opened his notebook and conspicuously poised his pen in his hand, assuming the look of a responsible religious journalist.

"Refresh my memory," he said, jotting down some numbers in his notebook. "Which one of you most recently quenched your thirst on a corpse by sticking a rubber tube up its carotid artery?"

In control now, he tore out the page he had been reading from scrapbook 100 and laid it on the pile of undertaker articles he had collected. He imagined Ody, Giles, and Washington in the coal bin with him. They tried to shift suspicion off themselves by encouraging him to read about lawsuits that had been filed against other undertakers. Jimmy Johnson, who was an auctioneer on the side and buried babies for free, had stolen Mrs. Whitehead's body from the Madison Funeral Home and Ambulance Service. Thorton Cheswick was sued by McDonald's for running a drive-thru mortuary forty feet from their drive-thru service window. Cheswick kept the opened casket conveniently turned to one side so the deceased could be viewed without leaving the car, but the McDonald's customers often confused the two windows and drove up to the wrong one. Thomas was so fascinated by these stories that he thirsted to understand and control death.

He turned off the yellow bulb, believing that he could embrace death more fully in complete darkness.

He moved his pen neatly over the lines of the notebook in front of him, even though he could not see them.

"When you die," he wrote, "you learn how to see colors in the darkness."

"Now," Thomas said, putting down his pen, "I am ready to wrestle with death head on."

To prepare for his imaginative battle, he took a long nap. He lulled himself to sleep in his usual manner, by imagining himself beneath an endless row of coffins, sliding effortlessly along on his back. He moved faster and faster, the undersides of the coffins clacking above him like speeding railroad cars. He counted each car as he passed under it, until his mind couldn't keep up with the numbers, and everything grew dark and silent and smelled damp. And he was asleep.

When he woke, Thomas consciously allowed his imagination to take over. He closed his eyes and saw himself standing at the end of a long row of open copper coffins. He looked down at Ody, Giles, and Washington, who were about to die, unaware that there were no undertakers left in the world to bury them. The three men thought they were merely taking naps in the coffins, comfortably sunken into purple velvet.

Thomas felt overwhelmed with inexplicable pity. "I will take care of you," he said gently. He was their comforter, their savior, their only friend in death.

The undertakers opened their eyes and tried to speak to him, with tongues quivering uselessly inside their swollen mouths. Their faces were unnaturally stretched and bloated, and the oily man had cut deep squiggly scars across their foreheads and performed a premature cerebral autopsy. Thomas had the impulse to cover their faces with the burlap sack. He fought back the urge to let his mind retreat into the safety of the basement, and called forth the image of the oily man as clearly as his thoughts would allow. He now believed that the oily man was death. He couldn't bring himself to smother the undertakers with pillows, so his plan was to allow the oily man to do it.

Far at the end of the row of coffins, the oily man materialized and encouraged Thomas to anoint the dying men by spitting on their foreheads.

"Forgive them their sins," he urged, his voice caressing its way across the valleys of velvet inside the coffins. "Use the Holy Patch. Pull it from your pocket and touch it to their temples. It will soothe them."

Thomas quivered with excitement and astonishment and, he feared, love. Here, before him, he had managed to conjure up his own personal Devil—his honey-voiced man who secretly seduced him with the power to forgive sins. If he listened to the man's whisperings too carefully, he feared he would lose the power to control him and somehow become his intimate. He wondered if it was possible to romance death.

He concentrated hard on the oily man's face, which unexpectedly detached itself from the rest of the body and panned forward to stare him down. The closer the face got, the more it blurred into a collection of lines and circles which were without logical form, without colors. And the more he thought about it, the more the oily man's face became his own. He understood the oily man now. He was not death. The man was his father, taunting him from the grave for the sins he had committed. He was the multi-numbered beast which could heal itself when sliced open. He was not an oily man at all, but a flaming mane of agony and four curved horns ready to pierce the flesh. He was all that Thomas could despise and submit to and adore and imagine simultaneously. He was the underbelly of Thomas's soul.

Thomas stood up, crazed, thrashing his arms aimlessly, and smashed the darkened yellow bulb against the ceiling, where it exploded and rained tiny splinters into his hair.

Frightened by the immediacy of the broken glass, he scrambled up the coal chute and pounded against the "Condemned" sign with his forearms until it broke free, then stumbled back out onto the street.

He wandered around the dark streets, certain he was about to die, and looked for a dramatic place to fall down. He had discovered nothing at all, he realized, except that his romanticism sought his destruction, and that the oily man had been born from his sins. He knew only that he was not his own master, and perhaps the oily man was in control. He knew only that it was time to die.

He walked until he came to an alley, overcome by the certainty that the oily man was waiting for him somewhere close by. The moon was behind him as he entered the mouth of the alley, casting a series of intersecting angles and cones along his path. He saw a dark figure curled up at his feet, seemingly ready to pounce, and fell forward in a terrified, exhausted faint.

Part 3—Purification

Vera woke up when Thomas fell into the alley next to her. She did not recognize him, but he had featured her in one of his "Street Smarter" columns and given her the nickname of "Vera the Cleaning Woman" which so many knew her by. Vera had been impossible to interview, because she never spoke to anyone and sometimes hit people on the head with her mop. But Thomas had studied her from a safe distance for two days, amassing relevant information for the column that featured her. The day after it had appeared in the paper, a small group of people gathered to watch Vera incessantly sweep the dirt, which they could not see, from the walks in front of Saint

Peter's Church. Occasionally she shook a squeegee at them and they crossed themselves superstitiously.

Thomas had written that Vera was really a saint in disguise. He knew that she spent most of her days cleaning the walks in front of Saint Peter's, or scouring her withered skin at the Allen Street Bath House. She kept a few mops, a squeegee, a broom, an ice chopper, and a snowshovel slung around her neck on four curved coat hangers, so that she was prepared for any kind of weather or harassment. Thomas had paid one of the gophers for *The Metro* to distract Vera so he could get next to her safely, close enough to get a look inside her bucket. The bucket hung from her belt by a brown shoestring and contained, when Thomas saw it, a scrubbrush, three sponges, a bottle of cleaning fluid, and a canister of tear gas, all neatly arranged in a circle. In his column, he had assigned religious symbology to each of these items, and hypothesized that Vera cleaned the walks and her body in order to seek purification for the sinners of the city. Because of the column, two religious fanatics who usually worked Wall Street together had doused Vera with a cup full of their urine.

One of the things Thomas didn't know about Vera was that she had stolen a key to the church which she swept the walks of, and she spent many nights sleeping in the back pew of Saint Peter's. She fell asleep by concentrating on the dense smell of beeswax inside the votive candles, which burned in tidy rows on narrow iron ledges in the back of the church. If none of the candles were lit, she dropped a coin through the offertory slot and held her face for a while over the candles after she lit them, wondering if she had the nerve to burn off her eyebrows. Vera like to fall asleep in the pew, not because it was warmer or more comfortable than the ground, but because the candles always made the air heavier and sometimes visible, and when she listened closely, she could hear the flames hiss softly inside their tiny glass cups. She had always wanted to live in a place where she could taste warm, thick air in her lungs every time she breathed in or out, and watch the world as it circled harmlessly around her, protected by a shimmering glass curtain which echoed her own voice and shut off everyone else's.

Thomas also didn't know that, because of the column he wrote, Vera had been tormented so much that she usually only cleaned in front of St. Peter's on weekends. She started an hour before each mass, and collected donations in a cardboard box covered with aluminum foil, which sat just outside the door for the parishioners to drop their coins into. During the week, Vera cleaned the alley just a few blocks from St. Peter's where Thomas had fainted. She methodically swept, shoveled, and sometimes chipped away the footprints of anyone who walked there.

Neither Thomas nor Vera knew that Father Jakes, the pastor of Saint Peter's, often sneaked into the church while Vera lay on the back pew. He alone knew that she was able to speak. He also knew that she sang a song about a place way up yonder top of the clouds with pretty little circling horses which children rode up and down on all day. This was Vera's vision of heaven. Her mother had taught her the song, and it was the only one she knew. She had forgotten all the words, so she made up verses of her own, not knowing if they rhymed or made sense. Only Father Jakes knew that Vera had a bad singing voice. In the church bulletin each week, he wrote a note to the parishioners: "Please drop a few coins in the foil-covered box on the way out. Help one of God's children who is not blessed with the power to speak His words."

Vera lay on her side in the alley, studying Thomas in the moonlight after he had fainted, wondering how he had turned all of the skin on his face into patches of black and pale green. She could smell alcohol from up to ten feet away, so she knew that he was not drunk, and she believed that he was not just pretending to sleep, because one leg was twisted unnaturally under him and both hands were shoved tightly into the same trouser pocket. Vera often found herself wondering if people were really asleep or not. In the morning, she decided, she would poke at him with a broom handle, pretending he was a dead bird, but for now she would watch his face all night to see if it would change into different colors or not.

When Thomas woke up, it was 6:00 a.m. and just getting light out. Vera had fallen asleep, but she still held her broom handle in front of her, protecting her face. Thomas lay there unthinking for a while, with a line of mucus from his nose dripping off the edge of one cheek, until he remembered how he had ended up in the alley. Just before he had fainted, Thomas heard the oily man whisper into his ear that he was about to use his synthetic hands to choke off Thomas's airway. He had fallen, clawing in his pocket with both hands for the Holy Patch, wanting to hand it over to the oily man and finally stop his whisperings and die.

Once he realized where he was, he recognized Vera sleeping next to him and remembered the column he had written about her. Once again, he thought, his life was taking on a pattern for his convenience, and it was his job to unlock the riddles set before him. Vera had shown up for a reason. Perhaps she was there to assure him that he had now become a street person. If he wished, now he could get his old job back and write a column about himself. Or perhaps she needed his help—she needed him to talk to her after years of scrubbing her skin apart without anyone important noticing. Or perhaps she was really the oily man in disguise. She had followed him for years and whispered in his ear whenever he allowed himself to admit it.

"Which one are you?" he said weakly, waking Vera up.

Thomas calculated that they were only four feet apart, their torsos parallel, and with a pencil he could have drawn a straight line connecting their brows. Vera stared him down without moving and pretended to be asleep with her eyes opened. She often practiced this, sometimes going ten minutes without blinking. The trick was to force her eyes open so widely that the pain reached down into her chest and became a part of her breathing, and then her eyes would refuse to close. Thomas could not distract himself from her insistent, meticulous gaze. She scoured his body without even touching him. She reached down his throat and squeezed his neck apart from the inside. She held him in her arms, rocking him gently. He believed that she was dead.

Then she blinked, and he noticed the sleepies in the corners of her eyelids. He realized that he was confused, and reoriented himself by thinking of her name. *Vera,* he repeated to himself again and again. He began free-associating with numbers, trying to get his mind to focus on the number of its choice. Long ago, he had realized that 22 was his most amicable number, and his mind kept returning to it, seeking familiarity. He did some quick figuring, using his own variation on the Hebrew-alphabet system, and was able to numerologize Vera's name into 8, 7, 5, and 1. In his head, he added the numbers and came up with 22, and it all made sense to him.

He sat up awkwardly, and Vera did the same, still holding her broom handle in obvious readiness. She believed that if she imitated his actions as if he were looking in a mirror, he would not realize that she was awake.

"I know you," Thomas said gently. "I named you. Don't be afraid."

Vera thought for a moment that she had seen him before, but couldn't remember where. So many faces, she thought, too many faces to remember which one was which. Sometimes the faces all turned into soap. She wasn't sure if this was the man who had been sleeping in her alley or not. His face had changed colors on her again, into unorganized pieces of tan and black and purple and red. She thought he was very ugly, but wasn't sure because she couldn't see past the colors.

"I have something to tell you," he said, and reached out his hand to touch her cheek. He imagined that he was mysterious and profound. He pretended he was a ghost. "I have sinned against you and everyone like you. I seek your forgiveness."

Vera slid back against the building, reaching behind a dumpster, and clubbed Thomas neatly on the side of the head with the back of her snowshovel. He slumped to the ground, bleeding from behind his ear, unconscious.

Then she ignored him for a while and busied herself with her morning routine. As usual, she had to slap the skinny Doberman pinscher that slept nearby across the nose with her broom, and she swept away his pawprints as he ran off. She was trying to keep the alley clear of tiny bits of gravel, but whenever she slept, more pebbles seemed to show up overnight, especially when it rained. She forced them into a pile and dropped them in the dumpster, using a shingle for a dust pan. The dumpster often came in handy. She gathered discarded bottles of dishwashing liquid from it which still had a few drops inside. She liked to squirt the liquid into puddles of oil in the streets to make rainbows.

In the dumpster, she found a long strip of blue ribbon and some twine, which she used to repair the side of Thomas's head.

He had made a small puddle of blood on her alley, and she didn't want to have to do any more cleaning than necessary. She knelt down and rested his head on her knees as she wrapped it. She made sure the ribbon blocked both ears, but left his eyes uncovered. Now, she thought, I am a woman who they think cannot talk, and here is a man who they will think cannot hear. She felt a strange sense of sympathy for him, perhaps because he had gone down so easily when she hit him, perhaps because they had stared in each other's eyes for so long. She looked at his repaired head for five minutes, trying to remember if she'd ever held a man's head on her knees before.

Thomas woke up and saw Vera's face above him, upside down. He began to sob without knowing why. Vera had fastened the ribbon around his head with twine, and as he touched the twine with his hand he thought it was his hair, matted with blood. He no longer liked being a street person. He longed to return to the coal bin, where he could imagine himself bleeding all he wanted without feeling any pain. Vera's upside down image jerked uncontrollably above him, and he felt sure he was about to die.

Vera found herself stroking his beard, and wished he would stop crying. She was excited that there was something new and strange in her life now. This was as intimate as she could ever remember being with a man. She lifted his head up and put him into a sitting position, then held out both hands to him. He needed her, she thought. She was his only friend in the world.

Thomas saw Vera's ice chopper lying just a few feet away from her, looked at her open, eager palms, and believed that she was about to gouge him in the stomach if he didn't give her some money. He still had money, he remembered, in his pocket, and he pulled out a handful of bills. Vera looked at the crumpled bills, eagerly clutched them in her fists, and slipped them inside the secret pocket of her coat. She wondered if he wanted to marry her. She held out her hands again, telling him with her eyes that she loved him.

Meanwhile, above Thomas's basement, two eleven-year old boys broke down Cyril Sanders' front door to earn their way into the East Tenth Street Goblin's Club. The president of the club had told them that a ghost lived in the house, and it was their job to break in and ask the ghost which club member was marked to die first. The answer would determine whether the boys were allowed into the club or not. They ran home after finding Cyril where he had fallen sideways onto the floor, frozen in a sitting position, obviously opposed to giving out any answers.

Part 4—Church

Vera carefully followed Thomas down the metal chute into the coal bin, wondering if she should talk to him. So far, he had been content to chatter away, without expecting her to say anything. He had told her that he was a famous reporter doing research for a newspaper, and he needed someone to clean for him as he worked. He had taken her into a D'Agostino store and led her to the aisle with cleaning materials. He told her he would buy her anything she wanted. Vera nodded her head whenever he touched something she liked the color of, and he snatched the item from the shelf and put it in his cart. He also took her to the aisle with canned goods, snacks, and light bulbs, so she would be able to feed herself and see the coal bin better as she cleaned. By the time they left the store, Vera had chosen, with Thomas's help, a pink light bulb, two cans of cling peaches in heavy syrup, a can of tomato soup, a combination can opener and corkscrew, a box of Appian Way Pizza mix, a bag of pretzels, a new bucket, two Palmyra scrub brushes, a bottle of Lime-away, Mr. Muscle oven cleaner, Lysol with pine action, Old English Furniture Polish, Scrunge dishwashing liquid, and a can of Tackle with bleach added.

In the coal bin, she watched Thomas screw the pink bulb she had chosen into an empty socket and turn it on. Now his face was a pleasant shade of red, and she smiled at him for the first time. Delighted, Thomas disappeared for a moment and returned to her, holding the burlap sack. With the corkscrew, he tore three holes into the sack and slipped it over his head, pretending to be a priest dressing for mass. He turned around in front of her wearing his sacred robe, and she smiled with approval.

Thomas felt giddy and made decisions impulsively, happy to have Vera as the first guest in his new life. He remembered his earlier decision to have a religious experience, and knew that she was somehow a natural part of it all. With Vera cleaning next to him nothing bad could happen. He was transformed instantly from sinner to saint. She would wash out any traces of the oily man from the coal bin, and his imagination would soar to new heights. She would guide him in his religious journey, and one day he would found his own religious newspaper, and give Vera a job as his star reporter. They would write side by side, fiercely competitive and happy. Thomas invented an entire past for Vera in his head, as she sprayed Mr. Muscle oven cleaner over the walls.

Vera felt equally giddy as she watched Thomas sit down at his table with the scrapbooks piled around him. For her, this was her happy husband who bought things for her. He wore a funny turban and robe and never expected her to say a word. She would clean their house while secretly singing to herself, and wait for the day when they would have a child together.

As Vera wiped the Mr. Muscle from the walls with a scrubbrush, Thomas eagerly reread the stack of religious articles which he had torn from the scrapbooks, waiting for inspiration.

He finally settled on an article about the Church of St. Peter and St. Paul in Manhattan, which a New York playwright and self-proclaimed priest named Bob Labar had made famous. In the church, Thomas read, Bob Labar conducted services in which the parishioners were blindfolded and forced to kneel at the altar for an hour in four inches of bread crumbs, then were ushered into a tiny bathroom for the environmental confession, where a smiling man wearing a wreath of toilet paper flushed away their sins—one flush for each venial sin and three flushes for each mortal sin.

Thomas tried to imagine himself attending services at the church, then shaking hands with Bob Labar, but he could not. He couldn't even remember any longer what the oily man looked like or what he represented. The articles he had just read, which once would have inspired hours of imaginative thought, were now merely words to him. His imagination failed him.

Finally, he reread the article on the Holy Patch under the light of the new pink bulb. He read that Christ had 125 welts on his body when he died. He tried repeatedly to connect his life to the number 125, but could not. He couldn't even remember the sight-cryptogram he had once assigned to the Patch. He could imagine nothing but darkness. Utter darkness, without colors or sound or space.

Meanwhile, Vera knelt next to him on the floor of the coal bin and scrubbed it with Old English Furniture Polish, watching Thomas's face lovingly.

Impulsively, Thomas fell to his knees next to Vera and made a confession out loud. He confessed to all the sins he could think of. He had broken nine of the commandments. He had taken change from his father's wallet, falsified his résumé, forgotten what a sin was, made up every word he had ever written, taken too long to grow up. He admitted to stealing the Holy Patch, pretending that numbers determined his destiny, relying on his imagination for food, and finally, he confessed that he had invented and given in to the oily man.

He knelt next to Vera with his hands folded, his chest heaving, begging for forgiveness. Vera dropped her scrubbrush and put her arm around him.

"You are my good and strange husband," she whispered in his ear.

Part 5—Imago

It was night. Thomas knelt next to Vera in the back pew of Saint Peter's. She had stuffed the bills he had given her into the offertory slot and lit all one-hundred and forty-four votive candles in the church. She stared at Thomas's face, entirely immersed and secure in the love she saw there.

Thomas, kneeling, gave his complete attention to the crucifix which was suspended above the altar, the candle flames scissoring fractured angles of light and shadow across the body of Christ. He gazed at Christ's face and slowly raised his chin without letting his eyes stray from the crucifix. He chose one point and stared at it continually, and his peripheral vision arced up and down along the outline of the body, absorbing it. He felt as though he was sliding closer and closer to the cross on his knees.

He whispered, over and over, the only words he could remember from a prayer he'd said as a child.

"They have pierced my hands and my feet. I can count all my bones."

Thomas felt his palms tearing where the spikes had been pounded through them. He had been stripped to a few rags, which slid down off his ribs as he grew thinner on the cross. He allowed his body to sink and bent his knees so that the weight was taken by his arms, but with his chest fully expanded he could not exhale, so he pressed up with his broken feet to try to breathe again, and his calves squeezed tighter and tighter, promising to stop him from moving altogether. He prayed that the Roman soldiers would come soon and smash his legs, so that he couldn't push himself up to breathe anymore. He prayed he would be given the strength to never move again, but remain choked and serene and dignified, waiting for the time when the healing would begin.

GOOD FOR RUNNING TO THE ENDS OF

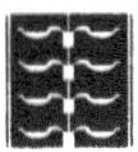

When he couldn't sleep, he liked to imagine being unmarried. Plucking items off the shelves as he saw fit. Black olives instead of green. Ground beef instead of celery and carrots. Complete freedom to smear raspberry gelatin over the face of secretary named Brenda or Kelli, her delighted giggles pillowing him back to the days before he had married Natalie, before all the talk of proteins and philodendrons, when women were girls damn it and eager to open themselves over him, like once-reliable umbrellas with broken handles that he just couldn't bear to dispose of because they were still so utterly, utterly practical.

They had two children. One Joshua and one Heather. Joshua was composing haiku in the fourth grade, and Heather could tap dance to the beat of "Hava Nagila." Joshua liked to lock himself in the bathroom, imagining he could play a guitar and sneer and smile like a rock star, while Heather pretended to have a Cairn terrier with a long muddy coat that she rubber-banded into braids. He encouraged both children to enjoy the house, which had clean oak floors and heated white ceilings, and two fifty-foot hallways that were good for running to the ends of.

Naked, he turned on the light and watched Natalie sleep. He reached a decision. He would change things. Force a pillow corner down her throat. Hang her by a necktie. Or weep—thinking that all he really wanted in the world was one night of restful sleep, and the promise that his bones, when he died, would turn to something other than ash.

www.ingramcontent.com/pod-product-compliance
Lightning Source LLC
Chambersburg PA
CBHW020926310726
48980CB00005B/403

* 9 7 8 0 8 1 4 7 7 9 1 7 0 *